He didn't want to open up his heart to God again.

He was still so mad at God, it hurt to even try to form a prayer in his head, let alone voice that prayer.

But tonight, he somehow found the courage to do just that. For Brittney.

"Lord, help me. Help me to be a good father again."

Because today, Nate had realized something so terrible, so tragic, that he felt sick.

He'd been ignoring his children, simply because they reminded him of their mother. He'd been a shell of a father, moving through each day with slow-motion efforts that sometimes took all his strength.

Until today.

Today, an autumn-hued angel had appeared on his doorstep and offered him a chance to find a little salvation. A no-nonsense, full-steam-ahead angel who'd somehow managed to be gentle and understanding with his forlorn, misunderstood children, in spite of her all-business exterior.

Which meant Leandra Flanagan wasn't always all business....

Books by Lenora Worth

Love Inspired

The Wedding Quilt #12
Logan's Child #26
I'll Be Home for Christmas #44
Wedding at Wildwood #53
His Brother's Wife #82
Ben's Bundle of Joy #99
The Reluctant Hero #108
One Golden Christmas #122

LENORA WORTH

grew up in a small Georgia town and decided in the fourth grade that she wanted to be a writer. But first, she married her high school sweetheart, then moved to Atlanta, Georgia. Taking care of their baby daughter at home while her husband worked at night, Lenora discovered the world of romance novels and knew that's what she wanted to write. And so she began.

A few years later, the family settled in Shreveport, Louisiana, where Lenora continued to write while working as a marketing assistant. After the birth of her second child, a boy, she decided to pursue her dream full-time. In 1993, Lenora's hard work and determination finally paid off with that first sale.

"I never gave up, and I believe my faith in God helped get me through the rough times when I doubted myself," Lenora says. "Each time I start a new book, I say a prayer, asking God to give me the strength and direction to put the words to paper. That's why I'm so thrilled to be a part of Steeple Hill's Love Inspired line, where I can combine my faith in God with my love of romance. It's the best combination."

One Golden Christmas
Lenora Worth

Published by Steeple Hill Books™

STEEPLE HILL BOOKS

Steeple
Hill™

ISBN 0-373-87128-7

ONE GOLDEN CHRISTMAS

A man's heart plans his way,
but the Lord directs his steps.

—*Proverbs* 16:9

To my nieces—
Layla Baker and Brittney Smith
With Love Always

Chapter One

Leandra Flanagan didn't know how her life could have changed so completely in just a few days. One day, she'd been a top advertising executive at a major Houston firm, making more money than she'd ever dreamed possible, and the next day, she was back in her hometown of Marshall, Texas, applying for the job of Christmas Pageant Coordinator for the city of Marshall.

She'd come full circle.

And she wasn't too happy about it.

"Ah, now, honey, don't look so glum," her mother, Colleen, told her, a hand on her arm.

That gentle hand was dusted with flour and cinnamon from the batch of Thanksgiving cookies Colleen was making for the church. That gentle hand brought some measure of comfort to Leandra, in spite of her own misgivings.

"Sorry, I was just thinking about the strange turn of events in my life," Leandra said, pivoting away from the kitchen window to help her mother with the leaf and turkey shaped cookies. "I'm just worried, Mama. I never thought I'd wind up back here in Marshall. I still can't believe I let you talk me into coming home."

"'The Lord will give grace and glory,'" Colleen quoted, her smile giving enough grace and glory to make any gloomy soul feel better.

"Mama, I appreciate that, but what I need along with any grace or glory is a good job. I had a good job and I guess I messed up, big time."

Colleen huffed a breath, causing her gray-tinged bob of hair to flutter around her face. "Sounds like you made the right decision to me, a decision based on your own values and not what your boss at that fancy advertising firm expected you to do."

In spite of the pride shining in her mother's eyes, Leandra didn't feel as if she'd made the right choice. But in the end, it had been the only choice she could make. She'd quit a week ago, and at her mother's insistence, had come home for an extended holiday, hoping to work through her turmoil before going back to Houston after the new year.

And now, her mother had gone and gotten the idea that Leandra could "fill in" down at city hall, just for a few short weeks.

"Well, no sense in worrying about it now," she

said, spinning away from the long counter where her mother had baked so many batches of cookies over the years. "I guess I'll just go and see what this pageant job is all about, at least earn some money through the holidays and keep myself busy."

"That's my girl," Colleen said, a bright smile centered on her round, rosy face. "Then come on back for lunch. Your brothers will be here and they're all anxious to see you."

"I suppose they are, at that," Leandra replied, grabbing her wool coat and her purse. "They probably can't wait to rub it in—about how I had to come home with my head down—"

"I'll hear none of that kind of talk," Colleen retorted, her words gentle as always, but firm all the same. "Your brothers are proud of you, and glad to have you home, where you belong."

"Oh, all right," Leandra said. "I'll try to pretend that I planned it this way."

Colleen beamed another motherly smile at her. "Maybe you *didn't,* but maybe God *did.*"

As she drove the few blocks to city hall, Leandra had to wonder what her mother had meant by that remark. Why would God in all of His wisdom bring her back to the small-town life she'd always wanted to get away from? Why would God want Leandra Flanagan to wind up back in Marshall?

Her mother would tell her to wait for the answer, that it would come soon enough.

But Leandra was impatient. She didn't want to wait.

"I can't wait for you to get started on this," Chet Reynolds told her an hour later as he shoved a stack of folders in her arms and directed her to a small, cluttered office in the corner of the building. "And first thing, ride out to Nathan Welby's place—it's the big Victorian-style house just out on Highway 80—and hire him on to build the set. He's the best carpenter in town—a single father of three. He works full-time in construction, but he's off for Thanksgiving this week, and he needs the extra cash. Only he's kinda stubborn and prideful, hard to pin down. Can you get right on that for me, Leandra?"

"Am I hired?" Leandra asked, still in a daze. They'd barely conducted a proper interview, mainly because Chet Reynolds had never been one to talk in complete sentences. He just rambled on and on, merging everything together.

"Why, sure." Chet, a tall man who wore sneakers and a Tabasco sauce embossed polo shirt, in spite of the cool temperatures, bobbed his balding head over a skinny neck. "Known your mama and daddy all my life, watched you grow up into a fine, upstanding young woman—that's all the credentials I need. That, and the fact that my last coordinator had her baby three weeks early—won't be able to come back to work until well after Christmas—if she comes back at all. I'm trusting you to do a good job on this, Leandra.''

So, just like that, Leandra had a new job. A temporary job, but a job all the same, based solely on her parents' good name and a little baby's early birth. The hiring process had sure been different from all the interviews and questionnaires she'd had to endure to land her position back in Houston. And the salary—well, that was almost nonexistent, compared to what she'd been making in the big city.

Good thing she had a substantial savings account and some stocks and bonds to fall back on. Listening to her father's advice, she'd built herself quite a little nest egg. And a good life as a *happily* single city woman who'd enjoyed pouring all of herself into her work. That is, until she'd gotten involved with the wrong man.

But that life is over now, she told herself as she squeezed behind the battered oak desk in the pint-size office.

"Must have been a closet in another life," she mumbled to herself. Dropping the folders on the dusty desk, she sank down in the mismatched squeaky wooden swivel chair. She hadn't seen furniture such as this since—

Since she'd left Marshall five years ago.

Putting the size and spaciousness of her plush, modern office in a high-rise building in downtown Houston out of her mind, Leandra spent the next two hours organizing the haphazard plans for the pageant. It was going to be a combination of songs and stories that would tell the miracle of Christ's birth, complete with a live manger scene—which meant that someone had to start building the elaborate set right away.

She couldn't put together a Christmas pageant without a proper set, and the entire production was already weeks behind schedule, and now with just a short month until Christmas, too. Well, first things first. She called her mother to say she'd have to miss lunch after all.

She was back at work and she aimed to get the job done. Her parents had taught her that no matter your job, you did the work with enthusiasm and integrity, and she needed this distraction right now to take her mind off her own worries. She would put on the best Christmas pageant this city had ever seen.

With that thought in mind, she hopped up to go find Nathan Welby.

It was the biggest, most run-down house she'd ever seen. And Nathan Welby was one of the tallest, most intriguing men she'd ever seen.

The house must have been lovely at one time, a real Victorian treasure. But now, it looked more like a gingerbread house that had been half-eaten by hungry children, a total wreck of broken shingles and torn shutters and peeling paint. An adorable wreck that begged to be restored to its former beauty.

And the man—was this the best carpenter in town? Someone who lived in such a sad place as this? He was sure enough a big man, a giant who right now was wielding a very big ax and using it to slice thick chunks of wood into kindling.

"Chet, you've sent me to find Paul Bunyan," Leandra muttered to herself. "Hello," she called for the third time.

The big man chopping wood in the backyard had to have heard her. But he did have his back—a broad, muscled back—turned away from her. And there was lots of noise coming from inside the dilapidated house.

Leandra had shuddered at all that noise. It sounded too familiar. Being the baby and only girl of a large family had taught her that she didn't want a repeat in her own adult life. She had no desire to have a large family and she certainly had no desire to stay at home and bake cookies and cart kids around to various events the way her mother had.

That was why her relationship with William Myers had seemed so perfect. No commitments beyond companionship, no demands about marriage and a family. William hadn't wanted any of those things, either. But he'd certainly asked for a lot more than she'd been willing to give in the end.

But she refused to dwell on *that* mistake now.

No, Leandra thought as she waited impatiently

for the man to turn around and acknowledge her. She only wanted to get back to her own plans, back to her civil, peaceful, *working* life in the big city, minus William's domineering influence.

And yet, here she stood, out in the middle of nowhere, about to hire a man she'd never met as carpenter for a one-month project.

Why had she ever let her mother talk her into taking this job?

She'd knocked on the heavy double doors at the front of the house several times before working her way around back. Music, giggles, screams, dogs barking, cats screeching—had she only imagined this house of horrors, or was it real?

Was he a real man?

He turned then, as if just now realizing someone was calling to him, and Leandra saw that he was very real, indeed.

Real from his golden blond wavy hair to the blue-and-red-plaid flannel shirt he wore, to the faded, torn jeans covering his athletic legs to the muddy hiking boots on his feet.

Real from the intense, wary look centered in his hazel, catlike eyes, eyes that spoke a lot more than any of the other noises coming from this carnival fun-house.

"Hello," she said again on a much more level voice, now that she was standing about ten feet away from him. "I'm Leandra Flanagan, from city hall—"

"I paid the light bill, lady," he said in a distinct East Texas drawl that sounded almost lazy. Dismissing her with a frown, he turned to center the ax over a wide log.

Leandra watched as he lifted his arms in an arc over his head, the ax aimed with calculated precision at its target, and in a flash of muscle and steel, went about his work.

The log split in two like a paper box folding up on itself. A clean split, with hardly any splinters falling from either side.

There was nothing lazy about this man, except that enticing accent.

Leandra swallowed back the shocked awe and justified fear rolling into a lump that felt as dry as that split log in her throat. "No, I'm not here about the light bill," she said, stepping over an old tractor part to get closer. "I'm here because—"

"I paid the gas bill, too." He turned away again, his head down, then reached to heave another log up on the big stump.

Off in the fenced pasture behind him, a beautiful palomino gelding neighed and whinnied, tossing its almond-colored mane and pawing at the dirt, its big eyes following Leandra.

Well, at least the horse had acknowledged her presence.

In spite of her frustration at being ignored, Leandra had to marvel at the sheer strength of the man. And the sheer brawny force surrounding him like an aura. He practically glowed with it, standing there in the fall leaves with the sunshine falling like glistening gold across his face. He was real, all right. A real woodsman, yet he was like someone who'd just stepped out of a fairy tale.

If only she believed in fairy tales.

He's only a man, she reminded herself. But so different from all the men she'd had to deal with in Houston. Refusing to dwell on *that,* she also reminded herself why she was here.

"Mr. Welby? I'm not here for any bill collecting." She waited, extended her hand, saw that he wasn't going to shake it, then dropped it by her side.

From inside the house, a crash sounded, followed by shouting and more dog barking. This caused the horse to prance closer to the fence, obviously hoping to get in on the action.

"'Scuse me," the man said as he dropped the ax and moved to brush past her. Then in his haste, he politely shifted her up out of the way as if she were a twig or a hanging branch.

He stomped up on the porch, opened the paint-chipped back door and bellowed like a lion. "Hush up in there. We've got company out here. Mind your manners, or you'll all three be washing supper dishes well into next week."

Miraculously, the music—a melancholy country tune—stopped in midwhine, the dog stopped barking and the screams tapered off to a few last whimpers of "leave me alone."

Even the big horse stopped his pawing and stood staring, almost as if he were posing for a perfect autumn picture, complete with a weathered gray barn in the background.

Then silence.

Silence over the golden, leaf-scattered woods surrounding the house. Silence as the November sunshine sent a warming ray down on Leandra's already hot cheeks. Silence as Nathan Welby turned around and stared down at her, his eyes still that wary shade of brown-green, his mouth—such an interesting mouth—twisted in a wry, questioning tightness that almost passed for a smile.

Silence.

"You were saying?"

Leandra realized she'd been staring. "Oh, I'm sorry," she began, then because she was at a disadvantage, having to look up at him, she took a step up onto the long, wraparound porch.

Only to fall through a rotted floorboard.

Only to be caught up by two strong hands, brought up by two strong arms, like a rag doll being lifted by a giant.

Only to find herself face-to-face—when she lifted her head about three inches—with those incredible ever-changing eyes again.

He settled her onto a rickety old wicker chair on the porch beside him, then kneeled down in front of her, his expression etched with a sweet concern, his long straight nose and wide full mouth giving him a princely quality. "I've been meaning to fix that. Are you hurt?"

Leandra brushed at her dark tights and pencil straight wool skirt. "No, I'm fine. Just a scratch, maybe."

His eyes followed the length of her leg, then he leaned over for a closer look. "Did it snag your hose?"

Clearly flustered, Leandra rubbed the burning spot on her calf muscle again. "No, really. I'm fine. Old. I mean the tights are old. It doesn't matter."

"Okay," he said, his gaze still on her leg. Then his glance shifted to her face and the lazy, easy-moving accent was back, along with the wry smile. "Now, what can I do for you?"

She at least now had his full attention. It was very disconcerting, the way he stared straight into her eyes, like a great cat about to pounce on its prey.

She brushed her suddenly sweaty palms across the tail of her tailored suit jacket, pushed at her chin-length curly brown tresses. "Well, I've just been hired as the Christmas pageant coordinator— for the city, you know—to coincide with the Marshall Christmas Festival. The pageant will be held at the civic center right across from the First Church—the big one downtown. The church sponsors the event."

Nathan Welby stood up then, crossed his arms over his broad chest and rocked back on the heels of his worn boots as he stared down at her. "Okay, and what's that got to do with me?"

She was at a disadvantage again, having to look up at him. And with the rich autumn sunshine streaming behind him like that—

She squinted, swallowed again. "I want—that is—the city wants *you* to build a new set. I've been told you're the best carpenter around here. I mean, I know you're busy, but if you could find the time, we'd pay you."

He kept rocking, his eyes never leaving her face, his whole countenance still and watchful, as if he were on full alert.

At first, Leandra thought maybe he didn't understand. She was about to explain all over again when a little girl with blond hair falling in ripples down to her waist came rushing out onto the porch, her eyes bright, her hands held together as if in prayer as she gazed up at Leandra.

"Are you gonna be my new mommy?"

Completely confused, Leandra could only form a smile and stare down at the beautiful, chocolate-milk-stained child. "I—"

"Brittney," Nathan said, taking the child up in his arms to wipe her face with his flannel sleeve, "this nice lady is Miss Flanagan from city hall, and she came to offer me a job. I don't think she's in the market for any mommying."

He gave Leandra an apologetic, embarrassed look, a kind of sadness coloring his eyes to deep bronze. As he held his daughter with one strong arm, he tugged at the gathered skirts of her blue denim jumper with his free hand.

The child, as if sensing that sadness, kissed her father on the cheek then laid her head against the curve of his neck, causing something inside Leandra's heart to shift and melt.

Then the little girl's next words, whispered with such an innocent hope, made that shift grow into a big hole of longing in Leandra's soul.

"But, I've been praying each and every night since Mamma went away and only just now, Daddy, I asked God to please send me a new mommy, so you wouldn't be sad and grumpy anymore, and so Matt and Layla would quit picking on me so much."

She turned to Leandra then, her big blue eyes, so different from her father's, so open and honest, so sweet and beseeching. "And now, here *you* are. And you're so pretty, too. Isn't she, Daddy?"

Leandra watched as this lumberjack of a man swallowed back the obvious pain she'd seen in his eyes. Giving her a shaky smile, he said in a husky voice, "As pretty as a little lamb, pumpkin."

Leandra's utter confusion and nervous energy turned as golden and warm as the sun at her back. If that statement had come from any other man, she'd have laughed at the hokey, down-home line.

But coming from Nathan Welby, said in that lazy drawl and said with such sweet natural sincerity, the remark became something entirely different, and took on an intimate meaning.

A meaning that Leandra did not want to misinterpret.

It was a compliment, said in daddy fashion to appease his daughter. Nothing more.

Apparently pleased with that answer, however, Brittney placed her plump little hands on her father's cheeks and touched her forehead to his, a wide grin on her rounded face. "Isn't she perfect for the job, Daddy?"

Chapter Two

Nathan looked down at his daughter's big blue eyes, so like her mother's, and wished he could feel good about all the hope centered there. Alicia's eyes had always reminded him of the sky over Texas, big and vast and deeply blue. Now, both his Brittney and her older sister, Layla, looked so much like Alicia it hurt him each time he came face-to-face with either of them. And he hated turning away from his own children, but that's exactly what he did sometimes—to hide his pain.

His gaze moved from his daughter to the woman standing in front of him. Leandra Flanagan's bewildered look caused her features to scatter and change like leaves floating through a forest. Yes, that was it. This woman reminded him of autumn—all golden and cool—whereas his Alicia had always reminded him of springtime—refreshing, colorful, blossoming.

Stop it, Nate, he told himself as he shifted his tiny daughter in his arms. Why did he always have to compare every woman who came along to his deceased wife?

Yet, there was something about this particular woman that made her stand out from the crowd. Only, Nate hadn't quite figured out just what it was, exactly.

"I'm sorry," he said now to Leandra. Placing Brittney down on the porch, he rubbed a hand across her wheat-colored curls. "Sugar, go on in the house now and let Daddy talk to the nice lady. I'll be in in a little while to help you with those leaf place mats you're making for next week's Thanksgiving dinner."

"Okay, Daddy, but don't forget what I said." Brittney gave Leandra another pleasant, gap-toothed smile. "You wanna stay for supper?"

The woman's expression went from baffled to downright panic-stricken. Nate watched as her big pecan-colored eyes widened. He could see by the way she was squirming and shifting, she felt uncomfortable with this whole situation. She'd come out here to offer him some much needed extra work, and instead had been asked on the spot to become a mommy to his children.

Something she obviously hadn't expected, or

wanted, and probably something she didn't run into every time she conducted business.

Well, he couldn't blame her for being a bit put off. Leandra Flanagan was clearly *all* business, from her spiffy wool tailored suit, to her dark tights to the expensive loafers covering her tiny feet.

But in spite of that aloof, sophisticated air, he liked her hair. It was a curly, chin-length golden-brown that changed color and direction each time she ran a hand through it.

And he kinda liked her lips, too. They were a pure pink and rounded. They fit her square, angular face perfectly.

Too bad she wasn't mommy material. Not that he was looking, anyway.

Wanting, needing to explain, he waited, his heart hurting for his child, for Leandra to answer his daughter's question. To her credit, she handled the embarrassing moment with savvy.

"That's awfully nice of you to ask," she told Brittney. "But I've already missed lunch with my four brothers. I think I'd better go on home for supper."

"You got four brothers?" Brittney held up her hand, showing four fingers. "That's this many."

Leandra laughed then, a genuine laugh that filled the afternoon with a lilting melody. "Yes, that's this many." She raised her own four fingers. "And I'm the baby of the bunch."

"I'm a baby, too," Brittney admitted. "Not a

real baby. Just the baby of my family. And I get tired of it, sometimes.''

Leandra bent down, her dark hair falling forward in a perfectly even wedge of curls as she came face-to-face with Brittney. "I get tired of it, too. My brothers love to pick on me."

Brittney rolled her big eyes and bobbed her head. "That's 'xactly why I need a new mommy. I get picked on, 'cause I'm the youngest and all. You could…proteck me."

"It's pro*tect*," Nathan corrected, "and I don't think we need to discuss this with Miss Flanagan any more today. Now, scoot. I'll be in in a little while, okay?"

"Oh, okay," Brittney said on an exaggerated breath. "Bye, Miss Flan-again."

Nathan saw the amused expression on Leandra's face, and relaxed a little himself.

"Well, Miss *Flan-again*, bet you weren't expecting all this when you made the drive out here today."

"No, not really," Leandra said, rising to face him, that curtain of hair covering one eye. "Your daughter is precious, Mr. Welby. And I'm flattered that she thinks I'm a good candidate…but—"

"But you aren't the one needing extra work, right? And call me Nate."

She laughed again. "Call me Leandra, and yes, as a matter of fact, I took this job because I did need work."

Her smile was self-deprecating. She looked uncomfortable again, standing there shifting her tiny weight on those fancy leather shoes.

Nathan noticed her lips, her smile all over again. While he enjoyed the attraction, the feeling also brought him a measure of guilt. He hadn't really noticed another woman this much, in this way, since Alicia had died. He couldn't do that to her memory.

Deciding to end this interesting diversion, he indicated the steps. "Care to sit a spell?"

"Sure." She joined him there, her hands pulling at her tight skirt for modesty's sake.

It didn't stop Nathan from admiring her shapely legs, though.

"Leandra, I appreciate the offer, but I'm afraid I'm going to have to turn you down on this job."

"Why?"

Her gaze locked with his, and again, he felt as if he were lost in a November forest full of sunshine and leaves and cool waters.

Before he could answer, three blond-haired children and a reddish-blond-coated, shaggy dog came crashing out of the door to fall all around them on the old, rickety steps.

"'Cause Daddy swore he'd never set foot in a church again after Mama died."

"Matt, that's enough."

Leandra heard the pain and anger in Nathan

Welby's words, but she also heard the gentleness in the reprimand to his son, too.

Watching as the beautiful Irish setter roamed the backyard and barked with joy at falling leaves, she wondered what she had walked in on.

This family had obviously suffered a great loss. His wife. Their mother. No wonder a sense of gloominess shadowed this old house.

"I'm sorry...about your wife," she said, hoping she wouldn't add to their discomfort.

Nathan glanced at the children. "You three go finish raking those leaves by the big oak, all right?"

"But Daddy—"

"Go on, Matt. And don't throw leaves at your sisters."

Reluctantly, the three overly-interested children trudged down the steps.

Nathan turned back to Leandra, his voice low. "Thank you." He looked away then. "She died three years ago, in a plane crash." His shrug said it all. "I guess I've got some reckoning to do. I haven't quite gotten over it."

Leandra's heart slammed against her chest and the gasp was out of her mouth before she could stop it. "How awful."

Then, the silence again.

But not for long. The three little ones were back in a flash, chasing the big dog right back up onto the porch, their eyes and ears set on listening.

Nathan didn't fuss at them this time. He seemed

lost somewhere else, completely unaware his children had stopped their chores.

Not knowing what to say, Leandra got up to leave. "Well, I guess I'd better be going. I'm so sorry I bothered you—"

"Wait," Nathan said, his big hand on her arm. "I'd like to clarify that statement, if you don't mind." Sending a fatherly glare to his three children, he added, "And if certain among us could remain quiet and use their manners and quit eavesdropping, I'd highly appreciate it."

"But we want you to take the job, Daddy," the older girl told him, her arms wrapped across her chest in classic teenage rebellion mode. "You need to get involved again."

"Yeah," Brittney added, hopping up to twirl around. "And we figured we could help out, too, so you won't be so scared about going back to church."

"How's that?" Nathan asked, a certain fear centered in his golden eyes.

Leandra knew his fear wasn't that of a coward, but of a father who was afraid to hear what his children might have decided behind his back, a man afraid of his own emotions, his own sense of unspeakable loss.

"I want to be the angel," Brittney said, flapping her arms. "Don't you think I'd make the bestest angel, Miz Flan-again?"

Her mind clicking, Leandra saw the opportunity

presenting itself to her. If she hired on the children, the father was sure to follow, regardless of his aversion to churches.

And a child shall lead them.

"You know, we do happen to have an opening for an angel," she said. "But have you had any experience?"

Brittney scrunched up her pert nose. "Once, when it snowed, I made angels in the snow with my hands and legs. Does that count—'cause it hardly ever snows here—and I don't get much chance to do that."

Leandra made a point of placing a finger to her jaw, as if she were deep in thought, although there was no earthly way she could have turned down this little girl. "I do believe that counts. If you've made snow angels, then you know all about the importance of this job. When can you start practice?"

"You mean I'm hired?"

"You're hired," Leandra said, extending a hand to seal the agreement.

"I'll be there whenever you say," Brittney replied, her big eyes shining, her small, slightly sticky hand pumping Leandra's. "I'm going inside to practice angel stuff right now."

"Wait a minute—" Nate said, holding up a hand.

"But, Daddy, you can't say no," the older girl told him. "And I want to sing." She looked at

Leandra with the same big blue eyes as Brittney's, although hers held that tad of attitude that just naturally came with being an adolescent. "I've sung some in the youth choir at church anyway, and they said they were looking for people for the Christmas pageant. I could help out there." She shrugged, just to show it was no big deal to her either way.

"Another experienced applicant," Leandra said, slapping a hand to her side. "We do need all the voices we can get for all those wonderful traditional Christmas songs. I'll let you know when we start rehearsal. And...I didn't get your name."

"Layla," the girl said, her eyes wary in spite of the tiny smile on her freckled face, her standoffish attitude breaking down a little.

"It's nice to meet you, Layla," Leandra said. "And I appreciate your offer to help."

"What about me?" Matt said.

He had white-blond hair and even bigger blue eyes than his sisters. And an impish quality that made Leandra think of her own brothers. He was probably walking trouble, but how could she refuse those big, questioning eyes and those cute dimples?

"What about *you?*" she asked, squinting as she leaned over to study him closely. "What do you think you're qualified to do?"

"I guess I could be a shepherd," he offered, his hands jutting out from his hips in a businesslike shift. "I helped Daddy round up some cows once that had strayed over onto our property from Mr.

Tuttle's land. And I was only around seven at the time.''

"How old are you now?" Leandra asked, caught up in wanting these children to be a part of her pageant.

"Ten. Is that old enough?" He asked it with such sweet conviction that Leandra knew she'd just lost her heart forever.

"As a matter of fact, I need a ten-year-old shepherd," she told him. Then she shook his hand, too. "You'll have an important job, you understand—watching your flock by night and all of that."

"I know," he replied. Then he rubbed the fingers of one hand with his other hand in a nervous gesture. "But I might need help with my costume. Our mom always made that kind of stuff."

Leandra swallowed back the sorrow she felt for this lovely family. "We'll find someone to help with that, I'm sure."

Having settled their immediate futures, Layla and Matt turned to go back in the house with Brittney. At the door, Layla whirled to her father, her long straight hair flying out behind her.

"Will you help, too, Daddy? Please?"

Nathan let loose a long sigh. "I need to talk to Miss Flanagan now, honey." When his daughter just stood there, her eyes sending him a beseeching look, he hastily added, "Oh, all right. I'll think about it."

That seemed to satisfy the teenager. She smiled

and went inside the house. Then Leandra and Nathan heard a loud "Yes," followed by laughter and clapping.

"I didn't get to interview the dog," Leandra said by way of cutting through the tension centered on the porch.

Nathan shot her a wry smile, then lifted his head toward the Irish setter pacing the yard again. "Oh, and I guess you just happen to have a spot for that big mutt, too. Maybe dress that setter up as a camel or a cow? Might as well throw in the horse—he'd fit right in in a stable."

"You're not pleased with this, are you?"

He dropped his hands down on his faded jeans. "Now what gave you that impression?"

"Oh, I guess the glare in your eyes and the dark, brooding frown creasing your forehead."

"Well, no man likes to be ambushed and sideswiped all at the same time."

"I didn't ambush you. I simply asked your children to be a part of the Christmas pageant."

He scoffed, held his hands to his hips, and looked out over the cluttered yard. "More like, they told you exactly what they wanted and you fell for it, right off the bat."

"Sounds like you've had experience in that area yourself."

He grinned then, and took her breath to a new level. She liked the way the skin around his eyes crinkled up when he smiled. He had a beautiful smile.

"I've had lots of experience being railroaded by those three, that's for sure." Then he turned serious. "It's just hard, saying no to them since—"

"Since their mother died. Nate, I'm so sorry. It must have—must still be—so hard for all of you."

"We have our good days and our bad days," he said. Then he motioned for her to follow him out into the yard.

"She loved this place. We'd just bought it, been here about three months, when she died."

"That's terrible."

"Yeah, terrible. Just like this place. I've been meaning to go ahead and fix it up, but my heart's just not in it."

"It's a lovely old house," Leandra said, her gaze shifting over the peeling paint and fancy fretwork. "It could be turned into a showplace."

"Maybe."

"Nate, if you don't mind me asking—how did it happen?"

"The plane crash, you mean?"

She nodded.

The silence stretched between them again in a slow-moving arc much like the sun stretching over the sky to the west. The air felt chilly after the wind picked up.

He looked out over the pasture, his gaze following the prancing horse as the animal chased along the fence beside the Irish setter. "She was going to visit her folks back in Kentucky. She hadn't been home since…since we got married."

Leandra sensed a deep regret in him, and a need to have this burden lifted from his shoulders. But she wouldn't force him to talk about something so personal.

And yet, he did just that.

"They didn't want her to marry me. I was dirt-poor and from Texas, after all. She came from a rich family—money, horses, all that bluegrass class. That's how we met—she came here with her father to buy a horse from this rancher I was working for and—"

"You fell in love with her."

"Yeah, from the beginning. But I was beneath her and I knew it. So did her folks. They gave her an ultimatum—them or me." He stopped, sighed, ran a hand through his golden locks. "She chose me."

He said those words with awe, a catch in his throat that only brought a painful roughness to Leandra's own throat.

"She hadn't planned on ever going back there, but her mother got real sick. They kinda patched things up and she was so happy. Couldn't wait to get home and tell me all about how her parents finally wanted to meet their grandchildren."

Leandra wanted him to stop now. She didn't

think she could bear to hear the rest of this tragic story.

But then, Nathan needed to tell it.

"They sent her home on their private plane—can you believe that—and it crashed in a bad rainstorm just before landing at the Longview Airport. Killed her and the pilot. We waited and waited at that airport, me and the kids, but she never came home."

And he was still waiting, Leandra told herself as she clutched her arms to her chest to stop her own tears from forming.

"I am so sorry, Nate." She placed a hand on his arm. "I didn't mean to dredge up all this. I'm sure you have your reasons for not wanting to be involved in church, but I'd love to have you working on this project with me."

When he didn't answer, she turned to go. To leave him to his grief and his memories. She wished she'd never come here. But then, the children needed to be involved, needed to have the support and love of a church family.

Maybe that was why God had sent her. Not for Nate. But for the children.

"Hey, Leandra?"

She liked the way he said her name in that long, tall, Texas drawl.

She turned at the corner of the house. "Yes?"

"When do you want me to start?"

"You mean, you'll do it? You'll build the set for me?"

He nodded. "Yes, for you...and for my children."

She stood there, her heart breaking for him. He didn't want to do this, but he loved his children enough to try.

"What was your wife's name?"

"Alicia," he said, again with that reverence.

"Alicia would be proud of you."

He nodded again, then dropped his head.

That beautiful golden silence moved between them, bonding them like a cord of silky threads.

"And what's the dog's name?"

"Mutt," he replied with a shrug and a lopsided grin.

She chuckled then. "I think I have a spot for Mutt, too."

"The horse is named Honeyboy," he told her. "I bought it for her."

She didn't have to ask to know he was referring to his wife.

"About this job—" he began.

Afraid he'd already changed his mind, she said, "You can start first thing in the morning, if that's okay."

"I'll be there."

And she knew he would.

Chapter Three

"**I** met the most incredible family today," Leandra announced at supper that night.

It was good to be sitting here, safe and warm in her parents' rambling home nestled in the heart of one of Marshall's oldest neighborhoods. This big oak dining table had been the center of many such family meals, and now with two of her brothers married and fathers themselves, more chairs had been added to the long table.

The noise level had increased through the years, too.

"What did you say, suga'?" Her father, Howard, asked, cupping a hand to his ear, the twinkle in his brown eyes belying the seriousness of his expression.

Leandra threw up her hands. How could anyone carry on a civilized conversation in such utter chaos? It had been this way all her life, that is until she had escaped to the quiet sanctuary of her own tiny apartment far away in the big city.

Looking around now, however, she realized she had actually missed the big family gatherings. She'd missed her brothers, in spite of their opinionated observations, and she'd especially missed her parents.

Her oldest brother, Jack, was busy cleaning up the spilled peas his two-year-old son, Corey, had just dumped on her mother's prized braided dining room rug. His wife, Margaret, was soothing their five-year-old Philip's hurt feelings at losing out on one of the drumsticks from the big batch of fried chicken her mother had prepared for the clan.

Michael, Leandra's next-to-the-oldest brother, was holding his six-month-old daughter Carissa, trying to burp her and eat his own meal at the same time, while his wife, Kim, passed food to their four-year-old, Cameron, and worked on crowd control so Colleen could rest for a few precious minutes.

Mark, the brooding professor who taught at Panola College and broke hearts on a regular basis, was actually reading a book and eating a chicken leg at the same time. No wonder the man was still single!

And Richard, only two years older than Leandra, was smiling over at her, his brown eyes assessing the entire situation much in the same way he watched over his customers at the old-fashioned general store he ran just outside of town.

Everyone seemed to be talking at once, except Richard.

"Tell us about this interesting family, Sis," he said now, his hand perched on a big, flaky biscuit.

Surprised that anyone had heard her, Leandra thankfully turned to her handsome brother. Richard had always looked out for her. "The Welby family," she said by way of an explanation. "I was out there today, and I hired Nathan Welby to build the set for the Christmas pageant."

"Oh, really," Colleen said, her gaze centered on one of Jack's noisy little sprites. Shoveling mashed potatoes onto little Philip's cartoon-character plastic plate, Leandra's mother didn't seem to be aware of anyone around her.

But Leandra knew her mother better than that. Colleen never missed a beat. She was almost superhuman in her maternal instincts and her ability to keep everything organized and together, in spite of the chaos surrounding her large brood. Leandra could never understand how her mother did it, nor why Colleen seemed so content to be a homemaker.

"Yes," Leandra replied in a loud voice, so her mother, at least, could hear her. "Mr. Welby—Nate—agreed to build a whole new set, and I signed all three children up for parts in the actual program."

"You sure had a productive day," Howard said, his gentle gaze moving down the table toward his only daughter. "Nate is a good man. He's had some bad times, but he's a hard worker. I talk to him in the bank every time he comes in.''

"Which is every time he needs to borrow more money," Jack, who was also a banker like his father, stated in his businesslike way. "I don't see how the man keeps up, what with the mortgage on that dilapidated house, those three kids, and with that huge animal to feed."

"Are you talking about the dog or the horse?" Leandra said, irritated at her brother's high-handed attitude.

Because he'd come from a good, comfortably blessed family, Jack had always held the notion that he was somebody special. And he looked down on those who didn't meet his own high standards.

"Both," he said, smug in his little corner of the dining table, his pert, pretty dark-haired wife smiling beside him. "The man needs to find a better-paying job and he needs to learn to control those three brats of his. Are you sure you should have invited them to be a part of the program, Lea? They can be very disruptive at times."

"Yes," Margaret, who always, always agreed with her husband, added, her nose lifted in the air. "I taught that middle one—Matt—in Sunday school last year—that is when he showed up. He was loud and unruly, not well-behaved at all. That man needs a firm hand with that little boy or there will be trouble down the road."

Leandra's guard went up. Bristling, she said in a

level voice, "Matt seemed perfectly polite to me, considering the sad circumstances. I just think the Welby children need some positive attention. The little one, Brittney, is going to be an angel. Layla will be singing in the choir, and Matt will be a shepherd."

"You'll regret that choice, I'm sure," Margaret said through a sniff. "He'll knock down the entire set."

"I don't think I'll regret anything," Leandra snapped back. "I think I can control a ten-year-old." When Margaret gave her a look of doubt, she sweetly added, "I did grow up with these four, after all."

"But you aren't married, and you can't possibly know how to deal with children," Margaret stated, her smile of maternal wisdom extending across the table to her own precocious five-year-old who'd insisted he wanted to sit by his nana.

The cutting remark hurt Leandra, but only for a minute. She'd long ago learned to ignore her sister-in-law's pointed remarks regarding her own often-voiced choice to remain single and motherless for as long as possible.

"You're right there, Margaret," Leandra replied in a calm, firm tone. "But I've watched Jack and you with your own children and I think I can safely say I've learned so much from your...uh...parenting skills."

As if to help his aunt make her point, little Philip

picked up his spoon and hurled it over the table like a boomerang. It landed, soggy mashed potatoes and all, right in his mother's lap.

Margaret instantly hopped up, an enraged expression causing her porcelain skin to turn a mottled pink. "Young man, that was totally uncalled for. Philip, that is unacceptable behavior. Do you hear me?"

Philip smiled, stuck out his tongue, then looked up at his grandmother with such an angelic expression that Colleen had to turn away to hide her own amused smile.

"Tell Mama you're sorry, sugarpie," Colleen coaxed in a grandmother voice. Then in a stern, firm tone, she added, "Philip, we don't throw spoons in Nana's house, okay?"

The boy looked sheepish, then bobbed his curly head. "'Kay, Nana. Sowee."

His sincerity was sorely questioned as he proceeded to mash his peas into a green, slimy blob with his balled-up fist.

Margaret turned to Jack. "Would you please talk to your son?"

Jack tried, really he did. "Philip, behave and eat your food, or I'll have to move you over here between your mother and me for a time-out."

That brought a pout and a gut-wrenching sob to Philip's upturned face.

"Now look," Margaret huffed. "You've made him cry."

Colleen soothed her grandson's feelings, and brought him under control, too. "Philip, we don't want a time-out, do we?"

"Nope."

"Then please finish your meal, so we can all have some apple pie."

The little sandy-haired boy turned demure as his grandmother smiled over at him.

"As you were saying," Mark called to Leandra, his book still open by his plate, his quiet, intelligent gaze falling across his sister's face.

Mark was so good at that, listening quietly, observing, taking everything in, even with his nose buried in a book.

"Oh, just that the Welby family is very interesting," Leandra continued, hoping Jack and Margaret would just stay quiet and let her enjoy what was left of her dinner. "And it's just so sad—about his wife, I mean."

Mark nodded, then pushed his tiny glasses up on his nose. "Alicia was a beautiful woman. And well-educated, too. We often talked about literature when I'd see her at church functions. She loved poetry."

Leandra let that tidbit of information settle in. So Nathan had married a beautiful—Leandra couldn't imagine her any other way—wealthy, educated woman who liked to read sonnets. Alicia was beginning to take saint status in Leandra's mind.

"How'd she ever hook up with the likes of Nate

Welby, then?'' Michael, who'd been quiet, finally asked.

"She loved him,'' Kim, his wife, said, poking him in the ribs. "It was a fairy-tale romance, from everything I've heard. She was lovely and he's sure a handsome man. They were a striking couple.''

Yep, that's exactly the way I see it, Leandra thought. Only now, Nathan was suffering too much to see his own potential, or that of his children. He'd let everything come to a standstill. His faith was in ruins, just like his house. Leandra wondered how someone could ever get through that kind of grief.

"Well, it sure had a tragic ending,'' Jack said in his superior way. "They were ill-suited from the beginning. I knew that the day they moved to town.''

Ignoring him and the hurt in her own heart, Leandra asked, "When exactly did they move here? I never knew them before and I don't recall running into any of them on visits home.''

She certainly would have remembered Nate, at least.

Colleen pushed her plate away and leaned back in her chair. "They came here a little over three years ago, I guess. Apparently, from what I've heard at church, Alicia Welby took one look at that old house and had to have it.''

"And Nate tried to move heaven and earth to get

it for her,'' Howard added. ''They came from Paris.''

''Paris, France?'' Margaret asked, her eyes brightening at the prospect. Margaret loved sophisticated people, and fancied herself one, from what Leandra could tell.

''No, silly,'' her husband retorted, rolling his eyes. ''Paris, Texas.''

''Oh.'' Margaret looked properly chastised, then shrugged. ''Well, I didn't know.''

''An honest mistake,'' Colleen said, amusement coloring her merry eyes. ''Nate worked on a big ranch near Paris, dear. But he took a construction job here, hoping to make more money. That's when they bought the house.''

''A few weeks after he started his job, though, Alicia was killed in a plane crash,'' Howard explained. ''And then, to top things off, her mother died—whether from bad health or heartbreak over the loss of her daughter—who knows. But I hear Alicia's father doesn't have anything to do with Nate or the children.'' Howard shook his head, then glanced at Leandra. ''Such a tragedy, but Nate put his nose to the grindstone and now he's made a name for himself around here. People respect Nathan Welby. They know they can count on him to get the job done.''

''He told me about his wife's death,'' Leandra said in a quiet voice. ''But he didn't mention Alicia's mother, or her death. I guess he and the grandfather don't get along, since he didn't say much about that either.'' She paused, then looked down at her plate. ''I think he works so much to take his mind off his wife's death, maybe.''

The whole room quieted after that. It was certainly a sad situation. Even Jack looked solemn for a minute.

''I'm glad you hired him, Lea,'' her father said as he got up from the table. ''Nate is a proud man, he's just lost his way, can't shake his grief. Maybe having something spiritual to occupy him will help.'' Then Howard turned to Colleen, ''Good dinner, honey. How 'bout me and these boys do the dishes?''

''Oh, how thoughtful,'' Colleen replied, her gaze locking with her husband's. ''You don't mind, do you, boys?''

Amid groans and whines, came the reply, ''No, Mama.''

Leandra had to smile. The love her parents shared was so obvious and abiding, it practically glowed. She loved how with a sweet smile and a calm, level voice they got their children to do things. And she loved the way they still called their grown sons boys. It was an endearing trait that somehow brought tears to her eyes.

She had to wonder what was going on right now at the Welby household. Was little Brittney vying for her father's attention? Was beautiful Layla pouting in her room? Was Matt getting into trouble? Was Mutt curled up underneath the dining table?

Would they have someone to say their prayers with them, to hug them good-night and tuck them in to bed?

Leandra hoped so, and then promptly told herself to quit worrying about the Welbys.

Looking around, she realized in spite of the noise and disorganization of a Flanagan family dinner, she loved her family and enjoyed being home with them, even if it was for just a short time. After the holidays, she'd have to head back to Houston, hopefully with another high-paying job lined up, thanks to her contacts there who had supported her decision to leave Myers Advertising.

After Christmas.

After she'd organized this grand production.

After she'd spent well over a month working side by side with Nathan Welby and his three lovely, slightly manipulative children.

Well, at least her time here wouldn't be dull or boring. She'd been worried that it would be hard to get over what had happened with William, hard to settle into small-town life again. But today had been filled with excitement from the get-go. Now, she didn't think she'd have time to dwell on the mistakes of her recent past.

Being anywhere near Nate Welby would cure that particular malady, she was sure. The man caused her heart to jump and her palms to become sweaty, for some strange reason. And she had to admit, William had never done that for her. He'd been a comfortable convenience, at the most.

Nate was anything but comfortable or convenient.

Probably because he was just so very different from any man she'd ever encountered. And probably because she was feeling such a sweet sympathy for his plight.

Just thinking about him, however, made her kind of tingly inside. Even now, hours after she'd left him standing by the fence watching his beautiful horse, his big hand centered on Mutt's shaggy back, Leandra felt a soft, golden bond with Nathan Welby. The feeling wasn't unpleasant, not at all.

Leandra looked up then to find her mother regarding her with a calculated little smile.

And silently hoped that her all-knowing mother hadn't read anything into this new development, or the dreamy expression that Leandra was sure had been plastered across her face.

He wouldn't get his hopes up.

Nate sat in the overstuffed recliner in the darkened parlor of the rambling old house, Mutt sleeping peacefully at his feet, and wondered if his luck was about to change.

He had lots to do between now and Christmas, at least. An extra job would mean even more time away from the children, but then they were used to his long hours. But he liked to keep busy, he reminded himself. He had calls every week for carpentry work all over East Texas, and he was next in line to be promoted to construction foreman at work. He liked to work until he was too tired to think, so he'd hired on with a construction crew that sent him all over, sometimes here, sometimes over across the line in Louisiana. But he didn't like to leave the children for too long, so he didn't take anything farther than driving distance.

But there was never enough distance between him and the emptiness he felt as he sat here each night, remembering.

Yet, he didn't take any jobs that would cause him to have to move away from this house.

Because he felt so close to Alicia here.

And because his children loved their home.

Since Alicia's death, they'd settled into a routine of just getting through each day, making ends meet, making sure they took care of each other. Now, Nate knew that grief-dulled routine needed to change.

Layla helped him out with the younger ones, but she was at that age where a girl really needed a mother.

And Matt, bless his heart.

Matt still missed his mother, still cried out for her in his sleep, even though he tried so hard to be a little man.

And little Brittney always seemed lost in a

child's world of make-believe, happy and chattering and content, too young to understand or notice her father's pain, or express her own.

Now, Brittney had announced that she'd been praying for God to send her a new mommy. And she'd decided Leandra Flanagan was the one for the job.

Why hadn't he noticed that his children were hurting just as much as he was?

Maybe because he'd made it a point to always find something to occupy his time. Maybe because he buried his own sorrows in his woodworking hobby out in the barn. Maybe because he just couldn't bring himself to think about it.

Nate felt the tears pricking at his tired eyes, and swiped a hand across the day-old beard stubble edging his face. He didn't know whether to laugh or cry.

Lord, he'd cried so many nights, sitting here in front of an empty fireplace, waiting, watching, silently screaming his wrath at God.

He was tired of the burden, the weight of his grief.

And yet, he couldn't let it go just yet. He was selfish that way. He wanted to blame God a little bit longer. It helped to ease his own guilt.

Thinking back over the day, he remembered Leandra. She was a pretty woman. Petite and tiny-framed, delicate, but so precise.

So different from Alicia.

Why did Brittney think a businesswoman, who obviously didn't have time for children, would possibly want to be her mommy?

Was the child just so lonely, so afraid, that she'd picked the first woman to come down the pike to be her mother? Were his children that desperate?

Or, had Leandra Flanagan come along for a reason?

Had God answered his baby daughter's prayers?

Nate sat there in the dark, wondering.

He didn't want to open up his heart to God again. He was still so mad at God, it hurt to even try to form a prayer in his head, let alone voice that prayer.

But, tonight, he somehow found the courage to do just that. For Brittney.

"Lord, help me. Help me to be a good father again."

Because today Nate had realized something so terrible, so tragic, that he felt sick to his stomach with knowing it.

He'd been ignoring his children, simply because they reminded him of their mother so much. He'd been a shell of a father, moving through each day with slow-motion efforts that sometimes took all his strength.

Until today.

Today, an autumn-hued angel had appeared on his doorstep and offered him a chance to find a little salvation. A no-nonsense, full-steam-ahead angel

who'd somehow managed to be gentle and understanding with his forlorn, misunderstood children,
in spite of her all-business exterior.

Which meant Leandra Flanagan wasn't always
all business. The woman had a heart underneath all
those layers of sophistication.

No one, since Alicia had died, had ever actually
taken the time to just talk to his children. Not even
their father.

But Leandra Flanagan had done just that, and had
pulled them into something good and noble, simply
by asking them to be a part of her show.

Nate wouldn't forget that kind gesture, ever.

"You don't have to hit me on the head, Lord,"
he said into the darkness. "I hear You loud and
clear."

Leandra Flanagan might not be the answer to his
prayers nor Brittney's, either, but the woman had
sure made him see himself in a different light.

"I'm going to build the set for this pageant,
Lord," he said. "And I'm going to do a good job,
but I can't make any promises past that."

Nate didn't want God to win him back over. He
still had a grudge to nurse, after all. He had to do
this, though. He had to go back to church. To pay
back Leandra for her kindness.

To make his children proud of him again.

And maybe, to bring a little Christmas spirit to
his own grieving heart.

Chapter Four

〜

"Okay, everybody, we need to show some real Christmas spirit here."

Leandra looked around at the group of people gathered in the civic hall to begin rehearsal for *One Golden Christmas*. While the event was being put on by the church, it would be held in the town civic hall to accommodate what they hoped would be a sold-out performance on Christmas Eve.

Smiling, she continued to explain how things would go. "I'm just here to oversee everything from rehearsals to ticket sales. You have a fabulous director. Mr. Crawford has the script all ready and you each have your assignments. If there are any concerns, please see me later. Now, I'm going to sit back and listen to Mr. Crawford's instructions right along with the rest of you."

Leandra took a seat, then turned toward the doors

at the back of the large building. Where was Nathan Welby?

Glancing at her watch again, she wondered if he'd changed his mind about building the set after all. If he didn't show up, she'd be in serious trouble. The set should have been built months ago, but it seemed as if everyone involved in spearheading this project had procrastinated until the last possible minute. She might wind up having to talk her brothers into helping out.

Well, at least Nathan's children had made it into town. All three were here, along with all the other children who were out of school for the week of Thanksgiving.

The Welby children had apparently hitched a ride with their neighbor, Mr. Tuttle, who was playing Santa Claus. And he looked the spitting image of Father Christmas with his white beard and rounded belly.

Right now, the children were being assigned to an adult coordinator who would oversee their costumes and rehearsal schedules.

Leandra groaned silently when she saw her sister-in-law Margaret taking the Welby children and several others over to one side of the center. Apparently, Margaret had volunteered to help out, since little Philip had a brief appearance in one of the production numbers. Well, she'd better be nice.

After making sure Mr. Crawford didn't need her, Leandra got up to go outside. Maybe Nathan was already here somewhere. Had she remembered to tell him where to meet her? Since the church was practically across the street from the civic center, she didn't think he'd have a problem finding them.

It was a crisp, fall day. Cars moved down the street at a slow pace, contrasting sharply with the traffic snarls Leandra had sat through on a daily basis back in Houston.

The air smelled fresh and clear. Leandra inhaled deeply, more to calm herself than to enjoy the weather. She was afraid she'd made a terrible mistake in hiring Nathan Welby.

But he'd said he'd be here.

That's when she heard the sound.

It couldn't be possible, of course. But it sure sounded like the clippity-clop of a horse's hooves moving up the street. The sound echoed loudly off the historic old courthouse down the way, then grew louder.

Leandra strained her neck, looking around to see what was making all the noise.

Then she spotted him.

Nathan Welby, riding Honeyboy, coming up the street as if he rode a horse into town every day. Looking just like a cowboy, coming straight in off the range. Looking mighty fine in his battered brown suede cowboy hat and flannel shirt. Of course, he had on jeans and cowboy boots, too.

And there it was again, that golden aura that seemed to permeate everything about the man. Or was it just that each time she saw him, she saw him in streams of brilliant light?

Leandra had to swallow. For a minute, she wondered what it might be like to be swept up on that horse and carried away by Nathan Welby.

Since he was headed right for her, the feeling grew. To defend the sudden overwhelming daydreams whirling like flying leaves around her mind, Leandra wrapped her arms across her midsection and waited with what she hoped was a professional look of disapproval on her face.

Nathan rode right up to the steps, slid off the horse with a natural grace, then tethered Honeyboy to a nearby iron bench before tipping his hat to Leandra.

"Morning."

"Good morning," Leandra replied, amazement fluttering through her heart as she watched him remove his hat and shake out his golden locks. "Do you often ride your horse to work, Mr. Welby?"

"It's Nate, remember," he told her as he stepped forward, one long leg on the step just below her, his hat in his hand. "Sorry I'm late. My truck wouldn't crank. I called old man Tuttle to bring the kids while I tried to get the thing to work."

Leandra nodded, then smiled over at Honeyboy. "Obviously, the truck didn't cooperate."

Nate gave her a slow, lazy grin. "Obviously."

They stood there, silent, for what felt like a long time to Leandra. Since Nate didn't seem in any hurry to converse, she tried to get things rolling. "Well, let me just go in and tell someone where I'll be, and then I'll take you over to the city hall work area, so we can go over the plans for the set."

He nodded, leaned back on his boots, kept the lazy grin. Then he said, "I'm gonna walk on over to the church and ask Reverend Powell if I can let Honeyboy graze on the back lot. Want to meet me there?"

"Sure." She whirled to go up the steps, very much aware of his gaze following her. Telling herself to slow down before she tripped over her own feet, Leandra burst through the doors only to find Margaret standing there, waiting for her.

"This will never do, Lea," Margaret said, her hands on her hips. "We have to talk."

"What's wrong?" Leandra glanced down the aisle where Mr. Crawford was talking to the group, going over the script and songs. "Is there a problem already?"

"Yes," Margaret replied, taking Leandra by the arm to guide her out into the hallway off to the side. "It's about those Welby children. They're already proving to be quite a handful."

"Why? What happened?"

"Well, that little one—Brittney—she insists that you promised she could be an angel, and I've tried to explain to the child that my Philip wants to be an angel. Whatever you told her, you have to change it. Give her another part or something."

"I will not," Leandra countered, her tone firm. "I told you at dinner the other night that Brittney was going to be an angel. You didn't object then."

Margaret shrugged. "I didn't want to bring it up in front of everyone."

Meaning she knew better than to bring it up, Leandra figured. Colleen would have set her straight right away, and Margaret knew it. Well, Leandra was Colleen's only daughter, and just as assertive. But not nearly as sweet and patient.

"Margaret, listen to me. I promised that child she could be an angel in this pageant and that's exactly what she'd going to be. I won't break my promise."

Margaret gave her an indignant stare. "Not even for your own nephew. Philip will be heartbroken if he doesn't get to be an angel."

Leandra lifted her gaze heavenward to ask for patience. "I don't want to disappoint Philip, either." Trying to figure out what to do, she threw up her hands. "We can certainly have more than one little angel. We'll have a whole chorus of angels, with Philip and Brittney being the smallest ones. How's that?"

Margaret didn't seem too pleased. "Well, I wanted him to be the *only* little angel. I just thought he'd be so cute, you know?"

Leandra had to smile. "He is cute, Margaret, and I'm sure he'll be a wonderful asset to the pageant. But I promised Brittney. Remember, Philip has a large, loving family to support him. Brittney deserves that chance, too. We can be her church family, and support her efforts as well.''

"Oh, all right." Margaret waved a hand as she pranced away. "But I'm warning you, I won't put up with any foolishness from those three country bumpkins."

Leandra had to check herself or she would have grabbed her sister-in-law to give the woman a good shake.

"Lord, grant me patience and understanding," she whispered as she pivoted to leave again. Then she remembered she was supposed to let someone know where she'd be, just in case any problems came up.

And with Margaret's attitude regarding the Welby children, Leandra knew there would surely be more to come.

Already, this little project was turning out to be more complicated than she'd ever imagined.

One of the main complications was waiting for her in the churchyard. Nathan stood talking quietly with Reverend Powell while Honeyboy enjoyed munching on the dry grass surrounding the prayer garden.

Why did her breath seem to leave her body every time she was near Nate? Why did he look so natural standing there, that enticing grin on his handsome face, his trusty steed nearby? Why did it seem as if she'd been waiting for just such a man all her life?

Ridiculous, she told herself as she made her way down the meandering pathway leading to the tranquil gardens and church grounds. Towering oaks swayed in the morning breeze, loosening yet more fall leaves. They made a swishing sound as Leandra trudged through them.

At least she'd had the good sense to dress casually today. Her lace-up boots, jeans and long sweater fit right in with Nate's standard attire. And Reverend Powell never bothered to dress up, except for Sundays. He, too, was wearing a flannel shirt along with khaki pants.

I could get used to this casual atmosphere, Leandra thought as the two men glanced up and waved to her. When she'd first gone to the big city, all she'd wanted was to be sophisticated and elegant. She'd abandoned jeans and flannel and anything else that might appear casual and country.

But, it didn't seem half-bad now. It felt right, here in this beautiful old town.

And casual took on a whole new look on Nate Welby. He could easily pose for one of her ad campaigns.

That thought reminded her that she was no longer in advertising. She no longer had the sophistication and elegance of being in the big city. But she would go back soon, she promised herself. And this time, she'd be a little wiser and a whole lot smarter. And successful once again.

After everything that had happened, she didn't feel so successful right now, however.

"Why the frown?" Reverend Powell asked her as he held out his arms to greet Leandra with a bear hug. "It's too pretty a day for that stoic face, Leandra."

"Hello, Reverend," she said, smiling in spite of her worries. "I'm just working through some concerns, but it's so good to see you again."

"Good to have you back home with us," the Reverend replied. "And in charge of the big pageant, too. You always did like to stay busy. But don't forget to enjoy this time with your family, too."

"She's probably frowning because of me," Nate interjected, a puzzled look settling on his face. "I was late to work on my first day. And I don't think our Miss Leandra here fancies people who show up late."

"You had a good reason," Leandra said, hoping to convey her understanding. "But I do hope you can get that truck fixed."

"It's just the fan belt. I'll pick one up at the auto parts store," Nate countered. Then he shrugged. "Don't worry, Honeyboy needed the exercise, and Mr. Tuttle hauled my tools in his truck."

Leandra nodded, then lifted a brow. "Remind me to thank Mr. Tuttle later."

Reverend Powell gave them an astute grin. "Well, I sure am glad to see Nate back at church for a change—horse and all."

Nate acknowledged that comment with a slight nod. Then he gave Leandra his full attention, smiling sweetly at her. "Ready to get started?"

"Yes." She turned back to the Reverend. "I told Mr. Crawford I'd be over at city hall if anyone needed me. I have my cell phone, but in case I miss a call, or you hear—"

"Don't worry. I'll take a message," the Reverend said, turning to head back to his office. "You two kids have fun."

Fun was the farthest thing from Leandra's mind. She felt Nate's presence as surely as the wind and the sun.

Business, she told herself. This is business. And she'd learned not to ever again mix business with pleasure.

"So, here are the plans. I'm not sure who designed the original set but the props are old and need repairing and repainting, and some of them need to be done over from scratch. We're way behind, so feel free to change things to suit your own interpretation—that is as long as it fits in with the script."

Nathan leaned back against the long conference table, crossing his arms over his chest as he watched Leandra. She moved around like a little bird, flittering and fluttering, fussing and fixing.

"Hey, calm down. It'll get done."

"Will it?" she asked through a laugh that sounded more like a choking spell. "I'm beginning to have my doubts. I don't know why they waited until the last minute to get going on this, but—"

"But it will get done," he repeated, looking down at her. "That is, if you relax long enough for me to ask you a few questions."

She stopped then, bringing a hand up to push that irresistible hair away from her flushed face, her dark eyes dancing to a standstill. "Oh, I'm sorry. What questions do you have?"

"Are you married?"

She skidded like a cat caught in a paper box. "Mr. Welby, you know I'm not married. I mean, your daughter asked me to be her mommy the other day and I would have certainly mentioned it if I were already attached to someone." She stopped, looked down at her boots, pushed her hair back again. "Well…you understand what I mean, I'm sure."

"I'm sure," he repeated, grinning. "Didn't mean to upset you. It's just that you seem so…single."

Leandra looked up then, giving him a chance to see the little flash of fire in her eyes. "Single? I seem *single*." She tossed her hair off her face. "And what's that supposed to mean?"

Nate turned to stare down at the plans spread out

on the table. The nativity scene, the Christmas trees, the stars, the doves and angels—all meant to be cut out of plywood—lay there in a flat uncluttered pattern against the table, waiting to be created, to be shaped into something special, something with meaning.

"You're all business," he said, still looking over the patterns and shapes. "All energy and fire. All stressed-out and high-strung. Most people I know who act like that are workaholics, and usually they're single since they don't have time for any type of personal relationships." He wanted to tell her he knew firsthand about working all the time, but instead he stopped, pulled a hand down his jawline. "And it just seems this project needs a calming touch. It is all about peace and tranquillity, after all. Are you sure you're up to this?"

She was mad now. He could see it in the little pink spots underneath the bridge of freckles moving across her pert nose. He could see it in the tapping of her booted foot and in the way she let her hands slide down to her hips in a defiant stance.

"I think I can handle things, thank you," she said, her gaze moving over him then back to the plans. "Back in Houston, I was in charge of several very large advertising accounts, Mr. Welby. National accounts."

She stressed the *national* part. "It's Nate," he told her. "Call me Nate. And I didn't mean to offend you. But, lady, you're not in Houston anymore, and you need to take a deep breath and learn to enjoy yourself.''

She huffed a deep breath. "*You're* telling me to enjoy myself. *You,* of all people? Don't you work a lot of long hours, too? Don't you have obligations, things that have to get done?''

"Yeah, I guess I do," he said, dropping his gaze back to the patterns. Well, she'd surely nailed him there. And he didn't have a quick comeback. Except to say, "But I don't get all flustered over every little thing. Mostly, I just go about my business, and I do take a minute here and there to enjoy life.'' Even as he said it, though, he knew that wasn't really the truth. And he knew he was picking on her to ease his own nagging guilt.

"That does it," Leandra told him, pointing a finger at the table. "I *am* enjoying myself, and my status, married or single, is none of your concern, and *if* I seem a little nervous, it's because I like having things in order and on time. And while we're standing here chewing the fat, things are not happening, Mr. Welby—''

"Nate."

"Nate. Nate! I need you to concentrate on making some sense out of this mess. Can you possibly do that for me? Can you actually get started on this—today?''

Nate lifted his hands, palms out, to ward off another tirade. "Sure. Sure. Just trying to help. Just wanted you to take it slow." He shrugged then. "I guess I just wanted you to know that it'll be all right. I'm here and I'll get my part done on time. And if you need help with any of the rest, just let me know. I thought after our talk yesterday, that we were friends, kinda.''

She actually looked sheepish, then her skin blushed like a fresh pink rose. "Well, all right. Thank you...Nate. And I'm sorry if I seemed a bit snappish. We are friends, of course, and I do appreciate your willingness to help." Then she whirled like a little tornado. "I think I'd better go check on the children."

"Good idea. I'll round up the plywood and my tools and get these patterns cut, at least. Check back with me in a few hours and we'll see where things stand."

But he already knew exactly where things stood between his new boss and him. At an impasse, obviously.

She nodded, already heading for the exit.

Nate watched her stomping away, then moved a hand over the pattern of a dove lifting out toward the heavens. "Well, *Mr. Welby,* you sure have a fine way with the ladies. Scared that one right out the door."

Which was just fine with him, Nate told himself.

He surely didn't need someone as complicated and high-strung as Leandra Flanagan messing with his head.

And yet, the scent of her perfume lingering in the air did just that.

Three hours later Leandra returned to the work space that had been set up for Nate behind city hall. With worktables and extra, needed tools provided by Reverend Powell and the city, Nate had gone to work on cutting out the patterns for the backdrop of the pageant.

But Leandra didn't find him working.

Instead, he was in the churchyard, apparently giving all the children a ride on Honeyboy.

And little Philip was up on the big horse right now, laughing merrily as Nate guided the gentle gelding around in a wide circle.

Frustrated beyond measure, Leandra felt her blood pressure rising. Everyone said Nate was such a hard worker. But did the man ever do any work!

Before she could scream her wrath, she stopped to watch Nate with the children. He smiled that lazy smile and cooed softly to Honeyboy, all the while assuring little Philip that he was safe up on the big animal. Even Margaret seemed to be grudgingly captivated as she watched her son's beaming smile.

"Hey, Mommy," Philip shouted, waving as he went round and round on the horse, Nate taking him through a slow canter.

"Hello, darlin'," Margaret called back. "I want to get a picture of you up there." She pulled a camera out of her big purse and snapped a couple of shots. Turning to Leandra, she said, "Isn't that just adorable?"

"Sure is," Leandra replied, her gaze scanning the crowd. "But Mr. Welby—Nate—is supposed to be working on the cutouts."

Margaret took another picture, then waved a hand. "Oh, he did. Look over there."

Leandra turned in the direction of the prayer garden, then let out a gasp. "Oh, my."

They were all there. The Santa kneeling over the baby Jesus, the angels, the doves, the Christmas trees, the squares that would become gift boxes. They had yet to be painted and decorated, but the patterns that had been flat and lifeless a couple of hours ago where now all cut out and ready to be finished. And Nate had them all lined up, as if waiting for her inspection.

"So the man can move fast when he has to."

Margaret lifted her brows. "What?"

"Oh, nothing," Leandra said, her gaze shifting back to Nate. "Just mumbling to myself."

Margaret watched Leandra as she watched Nate. "He's handsome, don't you think?"

"I didn't notice," Leandra replied with a shrug.

"Well, maybe you should," Margaret countered, an impish smile spreading across her porcelain complexion.

Before Leandra could find a retort, Philip called to her. "Aunt Lea, come ride with me."

"Oh, that's okay, baby," Leandra said, waving him on as she walked up closer. "You go ahead."

Nate turned then, his gaze sending her a definite challenge. "Oh, come on, Aunt Lea. You're not scared of horses, now are you?"

"Of course not," Leandra replied, acutely aware that all the children were watching her. And just to prove to the man that she could relax and actually enjoy herself, she strutted across the yard to pet Honeyboy. "I just don't feel like riding today, that's all."

"Nonsense," Nate said. Turning to Philip, he added, "Hold on now."

And before Leandra knew what was happening, Nate lifted her up in his arms and forced her up onto the horse, behind little Philip. She had no choice but to gracefully settle back in the saddle, the imprint of his big hands lifting her, and his face so close to her own clicking through her mind like one of Margaret's pictures.

While she glared down at him in shock, Nate leaned close, grinning up at her. "As pretty as a lamb and as light as a feather."

Leandra's mouth fell open, only to snap back shut. Oh, this would never do. How could she work with this man over the next few weeks? He was a major distraction.

And she did not like distractions.

But as she held on to Philip and let Nate guide them around, with all the children and their parents clapping and laughing, and Margaret snapping pictures, she had to smile.

And Nate smiled right back up at her.

Well, at least she'd managed to accomplish one of her goals today. She'd told Nate she was enjoying herself, working on this project. At the time, however, she'd been too keyed up over being around him for that to be a true statement.

But he'd done his work, kept his part of the bargain and all in all, things had gone pretty smoothly with the rest of the rehearsals and the million other things that had needed her attention. It had been a productive day.

So right now, she had to admit in spite of how the man made her palms sweaty and her heart shaky, she *was* enjoying herself. Way too much.

Chapter Five

The Wednesday before Thanksgiving dawned dark and cloudy with the promise of rain, which didn't help the mood of Leandra's little band of actors, directors, stage hands and general all-around volunteers.

The production was going well, over all, however. They'd gotten through the first few rough rehearsals enough to iron out the kinks and get everyone accustomed to their parts. Since it was mostly singing and a few one-liners, Leandra felt good about things so far.

When she *could* concentrate on *things*.

Never one to daydream, for the last three days she found herself constantly wondering what Nate had been doing. Had he finished painting all the Christmas trees? She'd better go check, just to make sure he'd capped them off with the glistening gold-tipped snow like she'd suggested. Or maybe he hadn't understood her instructions about the huge gift boxes. Maybe he wouldn't remember that she wanted one gold-and-white striped and another red-and-green edged.

Any excuse to just be near the man.

"I've really got to stop this," she told herself as she headed around the corner to just get a peek at Nate's work area—just in case he needed her—just to see what he was doing today.

What he was doing was sitting on a bench, just sitting there staring at his finished products.

Leandra had to give the man credit. He'd worked hard, and in just three days, he'd finished most of his assignment. She knew he'd taken some of the pieces home with him to work on at night. Layla had told Leandra this in a huffy voice, claiming her daddy had stayed out in the barn until well past midnight all week, painting "those big Christmas things." And just when he'd finally taken a week off from work, too.

Those big Christmas things now represented a beautiful backdrop to the pageant. In Nate's talented hands, the shapes and figures had taken on a new life. He'd taken the basic patterns and turned them into art—his colors were brighter than Leandra had imagined them in her mind, his angels more holy, his doves more alive with bright white-and-gold flight, his trees almost touchable, close to smelling like real cedar.

Everything was perfect.

Except the expression on Nate's face.

"What's wrong?" Leandra asked as she came to sit down beside him on the stone bench.

"I'm finished," he said simply, his tone quick and resolved. "Nothing left for me to do here."

"And that's a bad thing?"

He didn't look at her. Made it a point not to look at her. "I like to keep busy."

"Now who's the workaholic?" she asked, nudging him with her elbow, a teasing edge in her voice.

When he looked up, however, any further teasing remarks vanished. Leandra had never seen such a tragic, sad look in a man's eyes. It frightened her, touched her.

"Nate?"

"I'll be okay," he said at last, his hands clutched together almost as if in prayer, his head bowed. "I get like this when I'm done with a project." He sat silently for a minute, then said, "Sometimes, when I'm working on a construction job and we're finished—say it's a new house, I stay after everyone else is gone, just to get the full image of that house in my mind. But I don't see the wood and beams, the new windows and fresh brick."

He looked up at her then, his amber-colored eyes reflecting the storm clouds rising above them. "I see children running in the grass. I see a woman planting flowers by the front door. I see a husband coming home to his family from a good day's work.

Safe, warm, happy, together. That's what I see with each house. That's what I want for each house."

Leandra swallowed, but for the life of her, she couldn't tear her gaze from him. He'd just spoken of such beautiful things—the things most common people wanted in their lives—with such a great pain in his eyes, that it hurt physically to look at the man. And yet, she couldn't look away. And she didn't know what to say.

So she just sat there, her gaze locked with his. Then something passed between them on that stone bench, with all of Christmas spread out before them in golden bright colors.

Before she knew what was happening, she took his hand in hers. "Nate, I was wrong about you. I didn't think you'd get this done, but...it's absolutely beautiful. Everything is beautiful."

"And now I'm through," he said again, a trace of panic threading through his words. "Time on my hands."

And then she understood.

Most people who worked too much were working toward the future and success. But Nathan Welby was working against the past, and what he deemed his failure. Other people worked to brag, to validate what they'd accomplished, while Nate only worked to hide, and to forget what he'd lost.

And yet, out of that work, he created beauty. Only he couldn't see that. Or maybe he did; maybe it hurt him to see such beauty and know he'd lost part of his soul.

She had misjudged him. His slow and easy ways were an ingrained part of his nature, but he fought against that nature by staying busy with steady work that kept him from having any quiet time to remember.

Leandra longed to convince him that he had a future, a future bright with the promise and hope of his children, but she didn't know if she had that right, since she'd always put her career ahead of marrying and settling down. And she certainly wasn't the person to preach platitudes to him, since she'd made such a mess of her own life.

But she could pray for him, ask God to help this gentle giant, this sensitive, easygoing man, to find his way home again, for the sake of his children.

And she could quit looking at him as a distraction, and start looking toward him as a friend in need.

"Nate, I—"

Children, gold-hued children, laughing and shoving to reach their father, interrupted her next words. Layla, Brittney and Matt all scrambled around them like an explosion of bright burning sparklers.

"Daddy, I tried on my wings this morning," Brittney told him, hopping on his lap to give him a kiss. "They fit perfect-ity."

"They fit *perfectly*," Layla corrected, the old eye-roll exaggerating her words.

Matt clamored for his own bragging rights. "And my shepherd robe fit real good. Miss Leandra's mom made it for me. She's nice."

"That was nice of her," Nate said, a smile chasing the gloom away from his features. "And, Britt, I can't wait to see you as an angel, sugar."

"Can we go home now?" Layla asked, pushing long blond strands of hair out of her eyes. "You promised you'd cook a turkey on the grill for tomorrow, remember?"

"I do remember," Nate said, his gaze locking with Leandra's. "We like smoked turkey sandwiches."

"On Thanksgiving?" Leandra couldn't hide the shock in her voice. "What about dressing and gravy, pumpkin pie and cranberry sauce, all the trimmings?"

"We don't got trimmings," Brittney said, twisting to hug her father close. "We only got bread and turkey, and a bag of cookies."

"I'm not much of a cook," Nate said on a sheepish note. "Except with a barbecue grill, of course."

Leandra didn't know how the next words came out of her mouth, but somehow they popped out before she could think it through. "Then you can all come to my house for Thanksgiving. We'll surely have more than bread and turkey. And I know my parents would love to have you."

Amid the cheers and high fives of his children,

Nate gave her a look caught somewhere between panic and pleasure.

"Are you sure about this?"

"I'm not so sure about this," Leandra told her mother early the next morning. "I should have asked you first, Mom."

"Don't be silly, honey." Colleen moved around her big kitchen with the efficiency of years of putting on big spreads for her family. "We have plenty of food, more than enough, and you couldn't very well let that adorable family have sandwiches on Thanksgiving, now could you?"

"I didn't want that," Leandra said, shaking her head. "I guess I forgot how lucky we are, to be such a close-knit clan. Even when we fight, we've still got each other. The Welbys don't have anybody, really."

"Well, now they have us, thanks to your kindness," Colleen replied as she handed Leandra a dozen boiled eggs. "Make the deviled eggs for me, honey. You should be safe with that project."

Leandra made a face. "I guess I need to learn to cook."

"Might come in handy one day," her mother teased.

Leandra watched as Colleen mixed the ingredients for her famous corn bread dressing. She loved watching her mother in the kitchen. Colleen always had a peaceful smile centered on her face when she was cooking.

Leandra longed for that kind of serenity, wished she could be more like her mother, but it just wasn't in her nature to be...serene. She'd always been scattered, anxious, in a hurry. And for what?

What was she searching for?

"How are the eggs coming?" Colleen asked with a mother's knowing grin. "Now, don't worry about your brothers, Lea. This is my house and if I say we're having company for Thanksgiving dinner, then that's the final word on the subject."

"If you say so," Leandra replied, cracking and peeling eggs in a hurry. "But we both know they'll resent this—they do like to be clannish at times."

"Well, they can get glad in the same boots they got mad," Colleen said. "I'll have no fighting and squabbling on Thanksgiving."

"Who's squabbling?" Jack came in from the den, carrying a baking dish. "Here's the macaroni and cheese. Now what's up? You two fighting over deviled eggs?"

"No, we were just discussing dinner," Colleen told him as Margaret came through the arched doorway. "We're having guests."

"Oh?" Margaret gave her mother-in-law a questioning look. "Anyone we know?"

"I believe you do know them," Colleen replied, an impish spark in her eyes. "The Welby family."

Margaret's smile turned as sour as the pickle relish Leandra was dumping into the deviled egg mix. "What? Surely you're joking?"

"I don't joke about dinner," Colleen replied, her smile intact. "Leandra invited the Welby family here for Thanksgiving dinner, so Margaret, be a dear and set four extra plates—one at the main table and three at the children's table, please."

"You're putting those three heathens with my little Philip and Corey, and Michael's Cameron? They'll ruin the boys' dinner."

"How so?" Colleen said, her dark brows lifting.

"Well, I don't know. They'll probably throw food and…they might not have the best of manners. They are just so…rowdy."

"Then we'll just have ourselves a rowdy Thanksgiving this year," Colleen said. "Set the table, Margaret. Time is ticking away."

"Well, I never." Margaret slammed the dinner rolls she'd baked from scratch down on the counter. "Leandra, I don't know what's gotten into you. First, giving that little girl the best angel part, now this. What's next—you going out to their house to hang Christmas decorations?"

"Now there's a thought," Leandra replied dryly, amused at her sister-in-law's antics. "Margaret, they were all alone and planning on having sandwiches. How would you feel if that were your situation?"

Margaret held the plates she'd grabbed from the cabinet to her chest. "Well, I'd be sad and lonely, of course. Oh, all right, I guess what's done is done. We can't uninvite them, after all. But I'm going to keep my eye on those three.''

"That's the giving spirit," Colleen said, all the while stirring the big pot of dressing mix. "Now, troops, let's get this together."

With that, she started issuing orders to everyone who happened to walk in the door. "Howard, honey, could you make sure there's enough wood for a fire? And Michael, make sure we have enough chairs—get some of those foldable chairs from the garage, dear. Kim, you can mix the tea and make sure we have enough juice for the children. Jack, don't sit down just yet. We need you to check on the turkeys—they've been in the cooker since dawn—just about time to pull them off to cool down. Richard—now where is Richard?—he needs to put the ice in the coolers and get the drinking glasses lined up. Oh, and everyone, we're having four more for dinner. The Welbys are joining us, and I'll hear no protests, whines, moans, nor will I tolerate any rude, unneighborly behavior. Is that clear?"

Amid the nods, surprised looks, and "Yes, ma'ams" Colleen called out, "Oh, and whose turn is it to carve?"

"Mine, I believe," Mark said as he entered the kitchen and let out a long sigh. "Ah, the smells of home and hearth. Mom, you've done it again."

"What's that, son?"

"Made me glad to be a Flanagan," Mark said as he managed to sidestep several fast-moving bodies to give his mother a peck on the cheek. "Happy Thanksgiving, Mom."

Leandra stood back, in awe of the organized chaos surrounding her. At one time, she'd hated this—hated the house full of people, talking and walking all at the same time, hated being shoved here and there by too many brothers and too much commotion, hated not having a private moment to herself. But today, today, she was so very glad to be right in the middle of the Flanagan clan. Safe at home. Loved. Centered.

How had she walked away from all of this? And why?

She watched as her father held little Carissa and made the baby bubble over with laughter. Watched as Cameron and Philip ran through the den, little Corey right behind them, chasing a remote control car that threatened to uproot anyone who got in its path. Watched as Margaret and Jack chuckled and whispered husband-and-wife nothings to each other as they set the table together. Watched as Michael leaned over to kiss Kim, a special quietness in the look meant only for his wife. Watched as Mark recited horrible on-the-spot poetry out loud—"Ode to Giblets"—while he polished the carving knives.

Her family was quirky, unpredictable, clannish— and so special to her. And yet, she still felt set apart, detached almost, from the close-knit group. Where was the missing link?

Then she looked up to find Nathan Welby and his three children, huddled in the middle of the big den with confused, afraid looks on their faces.

"Nate," she said as she rushed toward them, so glad to see them here.

He looked directly at Leandra, then smiled that lazy smile. "We knocked," he said, "but I guess no one heard us. Can we come in?"

"Of course," Leandra said, smiling as she took the platter of turkey Nate had brought.

"Since we had it anyway..." he explained, shrugging as he handed her the heavy foil-wrapped plate.

"It smells wonderful," she told him. "C'mon in."

Layla and Matt hung back, shy, while Brittney rushed forth to get involved with the remote control car race. Philip immediately grinned at her and sent the car crashing against her white tights.

"Wanna pway?" he asked while he rammed the revving vehicle against her black Mary Jane shoes.

"Can I?" Brittney asked, her little hands on her hips. "Can I have a turn steering?"

"Guess so." Philip shrugged, then handed her the controls.

Nate smiled as they took off together. "Your nephew's a cuteypie."

"And walking trouble," Leandra said in a low

whisper, a grin covering her face. "But I think Brittney can handle him."

"She can hold her own, that's for sure," Nate replied.

Wanting to make them feel comfortable, Leandra urged Matt and Layla into the kitchen. "Mom, look who's here."

"Well, hello there," Colleen said, wiping her hands on her Kiss the Cook apron as she came around the long counter. "Nathan, it's good to see you again. It's been a while."

"Yes, ma'am." Nate extended his hand to Colleen's.

"And Layla, how are you, darling?"

"Fine," Layla replied, a shy smile turning her face from pouty to pretty. At Nate's pointed look, she added, "Do you need some help, Mrs. Flanagan?"

"How nice of you to offer." Colleen glanced around. "You can fold the napkins and help Margaret put them around the tables."

Layla nodded, then took the white paper napkins Colleen offered.

"And Mr. Matt? What would you like to do?"

Matt shrugged, then tucked his hands in the pockets of his baggy jeans. "I don't know."

Just then Richard came in, carrying pies and soft drinks. "Hello, everyone." If he was surprised to find Nathan Welby and his children standing in his mother's kitchen, he didn't let on. "Hey, Matt, Nate. How's it going?"

"Fine." Nate shook Richard's hand. "Need help there?"

"I sure do," Richard said, handing Nate a box. "I bake these pies at my grocery store and so I brought two to help Mom out. We need to pop them in the refrigerator." He turned to Matt then. "And buddy, I think you can set these colas on the counter then help me check on the turkey and ham—see if they need to come off the grill?"

"Sure," Matt said. "I love ham."

Much later, after all the greetings and small talk, Howard said grace, then the dinner progressed with lots of conversation and eating, one small food fight between Brittney and Philip, and then a whole lot of groaning from overstuffed tummies. When they were finished eating, Colleen gathered the older children up and took them for a nature walk in the big backyard, while Margaret and Kim got the little ones settled down for their afternoon naps. As everyone else gathered around the big television in the den to watch football, Leandra found herself alone with Nate in the kitchen.

"I'm glad you came," she said, then laughed. "Did I already say that?"

"It's nice to hear it again," he replied. "It's good to be around a big family. I—I never had that."

"Really?" Wanting to know more, she handed

him a slice of pecan pie and a fresh cup of coffee, then led him to a quiet corner of the breakfast nook where a small built-in storage seat was nestled underneath the bay window. "Where is your family, anyway?"

"I never really had one," he told her as he gazed into the leaping flames of the big kitchen fireplace, the music of a half-time show on the nearby television blaring in the background. "I—I lived in a children's home most of my life."

Not understanding at first, Leandra stared over at him. "You—"

"I was an orphan. The Children's Home took care of me until I was old enough to get out on my own."

Leandra felt that little warm spot in her heart growing to a fiery heat inside her very soul. "I can't imagine," she said, wishing there was something better to say.

"No, I don't suppose you can," Nate replied, looking back into the den where her relatives sat around in complacent camaraderie. "You're lucky to have such a big, loving family."

"I was thinking the same thing earlier today, but I didn't always think that," she admitted, mortified that she'd often wished to be an only child. "But I'm learning to appreciate them."

"That's good." He glanced back at the fire. "I used to dream of a family like this. Loud, noisy, pushy, fun. I guess that's why I don't always discipline the children the way I should. I like having them in the house, like the noise and shouting. And I like knowing they will always have a home. At least, I'm trying to give them one."

"You're doing a pretty good job," Leandra said, proud of his quiet strength. "Underneath all their bluster, they really are sweet children."

"All things considered, I reckon so," he replied. Then he said, "Hey, don't go feeling sorry for me. I'm okay. The people at the home were good to me until it was time for me to move on. I had some rough years as a teenager, but then I grew up and tried to be responsible, and for a while, I knew what it meant to have a real home."

"You mean Alicia?"

"Yes. She was my heart, my home."

He grew quiet then.

"Well, you still have your children," Leandra said. "They are so beautiful, Nate. And they are a part of you and Alicia."

Just then a loud crash from the front hallway, followed by a wail of childlike pain, brought them both to their feet.

"I have a bad feeling about this," Nate said as he urged Leandra toward the noise. "I think one of my beautiful little angels just destroyed something."

Chapter Six

"Well, we almost made it through the day without any catastrophes," Nate told Leandra an hour later as he headed his family toward his waiting truck. "And I mean it, Leandra. I'm going to replace your mother's vase."

She waved a hand in the air. "I told you, it was old."

He glanced up at the well-maintained white two-storied house. "Yeah, and probably priceless."

Leandra didn't miss Nate's wistful look or the resignation in his words. Based on what he'd told her earlier, he'd never had a home of his own until now. With a little fixing up, his home could be every bit as lovely and traditional as her parents' one-hundred-year-old rambling house, but Nate probably still wouldn't feel the kind of security her family had always taken for granted. That chance had been snatched from him when Alicia had died. It would be hard to make him see that most of her family wouldn't judge him as harshly as he seemed to be judging himself.

Trying to reassure him, she said, "No, it held more of a sentimental value. She got it from the local discount mart years ago."

Leandra didn't have the heart to tell him that she'd given the white ceramic vase to her mother for Christmas when Leandra was around twelve years old, or that it had been bought and paid for with ten dollars of hard-earned allowance money. That didn't really matter right now.

But it mattered to Nate.

He lowered his head, then kicked a cowboy boot in the dirt. "I don't know if I can find one exactly like it, but I'll come up with something."

"That's not necessary."

"I insist."

Leandra knew he'd make good on his promise, too. Nate had been embarrassed to find Brittney standing in the front hallway, holding the pieces of what had once been a white vase full of silk mums and fall leaves.

Before Brittney could stop crying and explain, Margaret had rushed into the foyer to grab little Philip, who lay kicking and screaming on the floor as he held a hand to the goose egg on his forehead.

After they'd all calmed down, Brittney had explained between hiccuping sobs that they'd finished their walk and decided to play hide-and-seek, and she'd accidentally bumped into Philip as he'd rounded the corner by the stairs. Philip had somehow been propelled into the round walnut pedestal table centered in the big hallway, and in an effort to stop himself, he'd grabbed at air. Instead, his hand had hit the tall vase, causing it to topple over and fall to the tiled floor.

Colleen had come up on the whole scene, explaining that Philip had run ahead of them, hoping to hide. But when he'd come around the corner, he hadn't known they'd be just opening the front door.

"You really don't have to leave," Leandra told Nate now, wishing Margaret hadn't made such a scene about the tiny bump on Philip's head. "Philip is all right. He's had worse scrapes."

Nate turned, a smirk on his handsome face. "Yeah, but your sister-in-law doesn't think too highly of me and my brood right now, so I think it's best we head on back home. It's getting late and I've got some work to finish up anyway."

"You said you weren't going to work today," Layla told him before stomping toward the truck.

Before Nate could reply, Brittney tugged at his jeans. "I'm sorry, Daddy. I didn't mean to bump into him. It was an...accee-dent."

Layla opened the passenger side door. "Yeah, and you're an *accident* waiting to happen. Get in, Brittney."

Brittney's blue eyes teared up yet again. "I said I was sorry."

"Brittney, honey, it wasn't your fault," Leandra said, rushing around the truck to take the little girl in her arms. "Philip said you were both running and that you just bumped together. You can't help it if he hit the table with his head."

"And knocked the vase over with his hand," Matt reminded them, clearly glad he wasn't the one in trouble this time.

Leandra remembered after the walk, Matt had stayed out in the backyard, talking to Howard. The two had hit it off immediately, since they both had a passion for fishing.

"I fell down, too," Brittney replied, her big eyes solemn. "But then I got up to pick up the vase parts."

"Are you okay?" Leandra asked, her eyes scanning the child for any signs of bleeding or bruises.

"Just hurt my bottom," Brittney admitted, her cherubic lips turned down. "I don't want to go home, though."

"We have to leave, sunshine. It's late and everyone's a little tired," Nate told her. "Now let Miss Leandra buckle you in tight. And tell her you had a very good time."

"I had a very good time," Brittney echoed. "And I still don't want to go home."

"Will you come and see me again?" Leandra asked, giving the child a peck on the cheek.

Brittney smiled, then giggled. "Can I?"

"Why sure you can."

"Nate?"

Both Nate and Leandra turned to find Colleen and Howard coming down the steps.

"Wait. I have some leftovers for you," Colleen told him.

Nate herded Matt into the truck, then turned to Leandra's parents. "That's mighty nice, Mrs. Flanagan. But I don't think I could eat another bite."

He rubbed his completely flat stomach, causing Leandra to wonder how the man could pack away so much food and still look fit as a fiddle.

"Then save it for tomorrow," Colleen said, handing him a grocery bag filled with plastic containers of food. "We sure did enjoy having you and the children over."

Nate nodded, shifted his feet, then said, "We had a nice time, too. And I do apologize for the broken vase."

"It can be replaced," Colleen said. She glanced at Leandra with her own apologetic smile. The vase had been one of her mother's favorite things, but Leandra knew that her mother put people and their feelings ahead of material things. "Besides, my grandson is just as responsible for breaking it, even though his mother might not see it that way. But I was there and one child was coming from one way and the other from another way and they collided. It was an accident, plain and simple."

Nate shifted his feet again, then nodded. "Well, I still feel bad about the vase. But I appreciate the dinner and the leftovers."

"Y'all come back any time," Howard said, shaking Nate's hand. "And don't worry about the vase or Philip. His head is as hard as a fence post."

"Is his mama calmer now?" Nate said, a hesitant grin splitting his face.

"Margaret's a bit high-strung, but she'll be okay. She's rocking Philip to sleep in one of the bedrooms. Too much excitement." Howard winked then. "And I think my grandson has a crush on your Brittney."

"She's a heartbreaker," Nate admitted, smiling over at his youngest daughter.

And so is her father, Leandra thought. Every time Nate smiled, the whole world seemed to turn golden and sunny. He should smile more often. *And I should quit acting like a silly schoolgirl.*

Howard laughed, then leaned into the truck. "Matt, son, I meant what I said. Just give me a call and we'll go down to the pond and do a little fishing."

"Okay," Matt said, a shy smile cresting his face. "Thank you for showing me your boat and fishing reels."

After a wave goodbye, Leandra's parents went back inside. And Nate was still smiling that lazy, knowing smile. It was a mixture of embarrassed pride and sincere gratitude.

The late-afternoon air was crisp on Leandra's flushed cheeks as she gazed up at Nate. "They really are glad you came."

"Oh, they're just being polite. You have a very nice family."

"And we're working on Margaret," Leandra teased, poking at his arm. "Guess I'll see you Monday."

"After work," he reminded her. "It might be seven before I can get there."

"No problem. We'll be rehearsing every night between now and the week before Christmas. So you can finish up the set and work around us, if you don't mind."

"I don't mind at all."

"And I'll have your check waiting for you tomorrow night," Leandra told him. "We appreciate you helping us out on your week off, Nate."

They stood silent for a minute, until Layla moaned and groaned inside the truck. "Can we just go home now?"

"She's pouting," Nate said underneath his breath. "Her siblings always embarrass her one way or another."

"She's at that age," Leandra reminded him. "My brothers used to embarrass me in the worst kinds of ways, too."

"They teased you a bit today, if I recall."

Leandra recalled, too. Somehow, her four brothers had managed to get in digs about her single status, her inability to cook, and the fact that she was very cranky in the morning. She'd be surprised if Nate ever talked to her again.

"Hey, I didn't believe a word they said," he told her now, his smile so sparkling and sure that she had to grin right back.

"Well, they were telling the truth—to a point. I like being single and I don't like to cook, but they exaggerated my shortcomings just a tad. I'm not too cranky after I have a cup of coffee."

"But you are a real city girl, aren't you?"

The question seemed so serious, she wasn't sure how to answer it. Maybe because right now, she didn't know the answer. She wasn't so sure about what she wanted from life anymore.

So she nodded. "Or so I thought."

He gave her a long stare, his bemused expression belying the serious gaze centered in his topaz eyes. "Right now, you look like you belong right here."

Leandra felt the heat rising to her skin, in spite of the cold November afternoon. "Do you think so?"

Nate leaned around the open truck door, close enough for her ears only. "Yep. You're all fresh-faced and dewy, like you've been on a long winter walk. You look like you're just waiting for someone to snuggle with on that window seat in your mama's kitchen."

Leandra became frozen to the spot, acutely aware

of his eyes on her, of his gentle smile, of his lips, his hand stretched across the door handle.

To break the magnetic pull that seemed to be bringing him ever closer to her, she laughed and tossed a curl off her face. "It *is* chilly out here. The fire will feel good when I go back in."

"Then don't let me keep you," he replied, standing back as if he'd just now realized he'd been flirting shamelessly with her. "Go on inside and get warm."

Leandra *was* warm, too warm. But she shivered anyway and wrapped her arms across her midsection. "Well, goodbye then. See you later."

"Later." Nate gave her a reluctant look, then slid into the truck with his children.

Leandra watched as they took off up the highway, headed toward home and what looked to be a glittering winter sunset.

And she knew she'd never look at the window seat in her mother's kitchen in quite the same way.

Nate looked at the birdhouse one more time. He'd finished it late last night, and he had to admit, it had turned out better than he'd imagined. But would it be good enough for Leandra?

He wanted it to be pretty—for Leandra and her mother. It was a gift to thank them for their kindness last week at Thanksgiving, and to replace the broken vase.

And a good excuse to see Leandra again.

Who was he kidding, anyway? Nate tossed down the paintbrush he'd used to put the finishing touches on the birdhouse. He wasn't in the same league with Leandra Flanagan and her family, not by a long shot. Being around her and her prominent, well-mannered family only reminded Nate of all of his miseries and shortcomings. Reminded him too much of Alicia's family and their disdain for their son-in-law. That disdain now separated his children from their own grandfather, Davis Montgomery.

He'd never been good enough for Alicia's father, especially since her death. Then after Mrs. Montgomery had died, too...well, the old man hadn't made much effort to keep in touch. Which just proved Nate surely wasn't good enough to become involved with Leandra, either.

And yet...

The door to the old barn creaked open then. Layla stomped in, slamming the door shut behind her. "I figured you'd be out here."

"Hello, sunshine," Nate said, feeling a little more than guilty for daydreaming about a woman he couldn't have. He placed the birdhouse back amid the clutter of his worktable. "What's up?"

"Matt needs help with his math and Brittney's been coughing and sneezing. I think she's getting a cold, not that *you'd* care."

"Hey, wait a minute there." Nate turned to face his hostile daughter. "Layla, want to tell me what's eating at you? You've had a burr in your bonnet for weeks now.''

Layla's sigh shuddered all the way down her slender body. "Daddy, why do you stay cooped up out here all the time?''

Nate glanced around, then back to his daughter. "I work out here, honey. You know that.''

"You work at your regular job, during the day,'' she retorted. "Then you head out here as soon as we're finished with supper.''

"I—I like working with my hands,'' Nate said, hating himself for the weak excuse.

Layla moaned, then turned to leave. "Well, it sure would be nice if you'd come in the house every now and then to check on your younger children. I get tired of having to be their keeper.''

Nate halted her with a shout. "Stop right there. Young lady, you are not going to talk to me in that tone.''

Layla looked down at the dirt floor. "I'm sorry, Daddy, but...it's the only way to get your attention sometimes. I'll go check on Britt, give her some cough syrup.''

Nate stared at her for a minute, hoping to decipher all the hostility he saw on her frowning face.

"Thanks, honey,'' he finally said on a softer voice. "I'll be in soon, I promise.'' He looked up at her then. "And Layla, I'm sorry, too.''

She closed the door and left him standing there amid wood shavings and power saws. But he knew she was right. He needed to learn how to just sit still and listen to the sounds of his children. He'd tried so hard to do just that, but somehow he always wound up out here, or worse—taking on extra projects that kept him busy at least two or three nights a week.

He'd been depending on Layla too much lately. Making her watch her younger brother and sister, making her do housework, probably making her life miserable in the bargain.

Now that he stopped to think about it, she really didn't get out much and do the things most teenage girls did, such as go to the movies or the mall, or have sleepovers. No wonder she was sullen and pouting all the time.

"I'll make it better, Lord," he promised. "Somehow."

Maybe Leandra could help him there. She knew about girls. He'd ask her about taking Layla on a shopping trip, let Layla pick out a special Christmas present for herself.

But ultimately, Nate knew the task of seeing about his oldest daughter fell to him. If he started depending on Leandra and then she up and went back to Houston, that would only make matters worse for Layla.

Which only reinforced everything he'd been thinking about earlier. He had no business pursuing a relationship with Leandra right now. Maybe ever.

Especially since he'd made a big fool of himself

on Thanksgiving by coming very close to kissing Leandra Flanagan right there by the truck. But she'd sure looked tempting, standing there in her baggy sweater and jeans, her wind-tossed hair falling across her freckled face.

He had to get over this need, this temptation to take things further with her. The woman had made it clear from the time she'd set foot on his property that she wasn't interested.

Yet…he sensed something there. It was in her eyes when she looked at him, in her smile when he walked into a room, in her every action. Was she fighting against this as much as he was?

And what was she really fighting? Leandra hadn't told him much about her big-city life or why she'd suddenly left it all to come home. Whatever had happened had apparently left a bitter taste in her mouth and given her cold feet about any new relationships.

He had to know. Wanted to know.

Maybe he'd just up and ask her.

Or maybe he'd just mind his own business and try to be a better father.

He looked down at the wooden birdhouse, thinking it wasn't good enough. Nothing he'd ever done had been good enough.

But right now, it was all he had to give.

"Can you stop by my truck?" Nate asked Leandra the next night after rehearsal. "I have something for you."

Leandra swallowed back the surprise she felt. He'd been avoiding her since Thanksgiving. And now he had something to give her.

"What is it?" she asked, wondering why Nate had seemed so distant over the past few days.

They'd worked together, getting the set ready for dress rehearsals. The props looked great and Nate had just about finished designing the entire set. After Nate was done with his official chores each night, he'd sit and watch the production, or sometimes he'd wander off into the night. Several times, she'd found him outside, gazing at the stars. Sometimes she'd find him talking quietly to Reverend Powell.

That, of course, was a good sign and might explain his distance and quiet aloofness. Maybe Nate was wrestling with his faith; maybe he was quietly coming to a change in his life. And maybe that meant he didn't want any distractions from her.

"Nate," she said now, "what do you have for me? Another prop? Another complaint from Margaret? Or did you ride your horse to work again?"

"Nope, I didn't bring Honeyboy this time." His smile broke the tension lining his face. "I've finished most of the props and thankfully, Margaret hasn't had one complaint tonight, but hey, the night's young, right?"

Leandra laughed. His sense of humor might be dry and unexpected, but Nate got in his own zingers when he wanted to. And he was obviously beginning to understand that her high-strung, well-meaning sister-in-law would probably never be satisfied with anything in life.

"Margaret would complain if the moon shifted," Leandra said in a whisper, "but some people are happy even when they whine their way through life."

Nate nodded. "I know. And she was as cute as a button when she stomped that little foot the other night and demanded to know who stole Philip's angel wings."

"We had to break it to her gently that the angel himself left his wings in the little boys' room." Leandra grinned, then shook her head. "Even angels have to go to the bathroom sometimes."

Changing the subject, she poked at Nate's arm. "Okay, so what's this big surprise in your truck?"

"C'mon and I'll show you," he told her as he took her by the hand. "And hurry before my kids come charging out the door."

Realizing they'd be alone near the moonlit prayer garden, Leandra had to take a deep, calming breath. She'd never been alone in the dark with Nate, but she sure had thought about being alone with him. A lot.

"They're having cookies and hot chocolate," she managed to pant out. "They should be out in a few minutes."

"This won't take long," he said as they reached the truck. "I made you and your mama a little something, just to replace the vase."

Leandra watched as he hauled a bag out of the back of the pickup. "Nate, I told you—"

Whatever protest she'd been about to mount ended when she saw the object he offered over to her.

It was the most beautiful birdhouse she'd ever seen.

Chapter Seven

Leandra took the delicate wooden birdhouse in her hands, holding it up to the nearby streetlight so she could see the intricate design better.

"Nate, this is so pretty. Where did you get it?"

When he looked down, then shifted his booted feet, she suddenly realized he hadn't bought it.

"You made this?"

He nodded, still looking at the ground. "It's not a vase, but I thought it might be pretty sitting on your mama's hall table during Christmas."

"Absolutely," she replied, silly tears springing to her eyes. "She's going to love this."

"It's no big deal," he said, looking up at her at last. "I just wanted to do something to thank you both for your kindness."

Leandra turned the birdhouse around in her hands so she could again hold it up to the streetlight just over their heads, careful not to drop it on the concrete. It was about a foot wide at the top and just as tall, made of what looked like pinewood. The roof slanted down in an inverted V-shape to cover the square base. The whole thing had been varnished and lacquered until it shined, but what really caught her attention was the detailing.

The slanted roof was shingled with dainty little wood cutouts tipped in white paint that sparkled like freshly fallen snow. The door and two side windows held intricately designed wooden shutters also touched with brilliant white icicles. There was even a smaller window just below the roof, right above the little open door, which had a small window box complete with flowing ivy. And all around the roof, the snow-tipped eaves had been painted with tiny red poinsettias and holly berries, set against little green magnolia leaves.

It was exquisite.

"It reminds me of a cuckoo clock," she said.

"Without the cuckoo," Nate replied, smiling sheepishly. "I'm glad you like it."

"I love it," Leandra said, a catch in her voice. "How did you make all the little curlicues and swirls around the openings and roof? And the snow and flowers—they look so real."

"I have all kinds of jigsaws and sometimes I carve pieces by hand. I paint the designs on."

"Amazing. Sounds as if this isn't your first effort."

"I've made a few," he admitted. "It's just a hobby. Something to pass the time. I'm working on a version for each season of the year."

Leandra carefully placed the delicate house back in the bag. "This is much prettier than that old vase. My mother will be thrilled. I'll go put it in my car right now."

Nate took the bag from her. "Here, let's put it back in the truck for now." He placed the bag inside on the driver's seat. "Want to go for a walk?"

Caught completely off guard, Leandra didn't have time to come up with all the excuses she needed to refuse. "Sure."

He took her to the prayer garden in the churchyard just opposite the civic center.

But then, she'd known that's where he was going to take her, at least had hoped he'd do so.

"It's a pretty night," Nate said as he pulled her to a wooden bench with a tall, spindled back. "I like the quiet...sometimes."

"Me, too," she said, wondering what the "sometimes" meant. "These rehearsals sure do get noisy and disorganized. It's nice to find a moment to just sit."

"You're doing a good job, bringing all these folks together."

"I've had a lot of help," she told him. Sensing his need to talk, she prattled on herself. "You know, this production started as a small play in the church fellowship hall. But it became so popular, with so many people coming, they had to add extra performances and move it to the civic center.''

"Well, the Wonderland of Lights sure brings in a lot of tourists.''

Leandra looked down the street where millions of tiny white lights blinked and twinkled on the old courthouse centered in the middle of town. The Wonderland of Lights brought in thousands of people each year from Thanksgiving until New Year's Eve, and this year had been no exception. Already, Leandra had seen the buses and cars full of people coming each night to see the awesome Christmas decorations.

Not only was the courthouse strung with over 250 thousand lights, but just about every other building in Marshall, both commercial and residential, was also decorated. The civic center was decked in bright colorful lighted cutouts, and the church held a breathtaking lighted cross. There was also a lighted star over a nativity scene made completely from white wire figurines covered with the same tiny white lights that were hanging all over town. It was a Marshall tradition that had made the city famous throughout the world. Even the trees glistened with starlike white lights.

"It's impressive," Leandra said, remembering how she'd always enjoyed the lighted city during the Christmas season each year. "Have you and the children taken the official sightseeing tour yet?''

"No. I've been so busy—" He stopped, looked at the lights. "Guess I'll have to make time."

Leandra shivered as a cold night wind whipped around the corner. "The temperature's dropping."

Nate took off his lightweight denim barn jacket and wrapped it around her. "How's that?"

"Better," she said as she looked up at him. Even better than better, she thought to herself. The jacket still held his body warmth and the clean, woodsy scent of whatever soap he had used that day. She'd like to buy a gallon of the stuff, whatever it was.

Nate glanced over at her, his catlike eyes appraising her with that lazy, I'm-taking-my-own-sweet-time way. "You're almost lost in there."

"You're a lot taller than me," she said by way of explanation. "Thanks, though."

"You're welcome—though."

His eyes held hers, shimmering as brightly as any Christmas lights she'd seen. Mercy, when Nate Welby set his mind on flirting, it made her insides curl into ribbons of fire. She was very glad she was sitting down.

Then he tilted his head, his eyes centered on her face.

"You didn't thank me properly for the birdhouse," he said, his voice as gravelly as the pebbles beneath their feet.

"I didn't say thank you?" she asked, acutely aware of how he'd managed to wrap a long arm around her neck.

"You might have, but I was kinda hoping for a hug or maybe a peck on the cheek."

"Really?"

"Really."

"Is that why you brought me to this secluded bench?"

"Maybe." He shrugged, turning serious. "Or maybe I just wanted some peace and quiet."

"It's up to you," Leandra said, meaning it.

If Nate Welby wanted to kiss her, she wouldn't stop him, couldn't if her heart depended on it. But she wouldn't push him into something he might regret either. Because her heart also depended on that not happening. She couldn't bear his regrets.

"I reckon you're right there," he said. "Maybe I won't find any peace until I have kissed you."

Then he pulled her head around, his fingers gentle on her cheekbone, and touched his lips to hers, tentatively at first. After lifting his head to gauge her reaction, he kissed her again. This one took a little longer.

"You're welcome," he said as he let her go, his eyes holding hers in the glittering moonlight.

Leandra felt as if she'd been in a snowstorm and was now melting in a puddle of heat like Frosty the Snowman. Nate's kiss had dissolved her completely, making her a pile of helpless mush.

But apparently it hadn't brought him that peace he was seeking.

"I shouldn't have done that," he said as he stood

up and pulled her with him. "I told myself not to do that, and look at me. I went and did it anyway."

Confused and hurt, Leandra asked, "Was kissing me that painful?"

He turned then, taking her back in his arms. "No, Leandra, it was that good. Too good."

"You're afraid of me, aren't you?" she asked, her tone full of disappointment.

"Yes, I guess I am," he admitted, his hand coming up to cup her chin. "But more than that, I'm afraid of myself. I don't want to mislead you, and I sure don't want to hurt you."

"Because you're not over Alicia?"

"Because I never did right by Alicia, and I don't know if I could do right by you."

Leandra's frustration brought her back to reality.

"That's ridiculous. You have to stop blaming yourself, Nate. If you don't, you'll never find any peace, any happiness."

"Maybe that's my punishment."

"Only if you let it be."

Then he turned the tables on her. "Yeah, well, what's your excuse? You left Houston for some reason. Want to tell me about that?"

"No, I don't," she said, thinking he sure would go to any lengths to take the attention away from his own problems.

Then he surprised her yet again. "I'd really like to know."

The soft edge in his husky voice almost did her

in. But she wasn't ready to tell him the whole sordid story. "Let's just say that I had no choice."

Leandra could see the determination in his eyes, even in the muted moonlight. Nate wasn't going to let this go so easily.

"You left a high-paying job to come back home. That right there shows it must have been pretty bad. What with you being such a gung ho city girl and all."

Now he was becoming downright sarcastic. "Nate, I didn't just leave a job," she blurted out. "I left a bad relationship with an older man who happened to be my boss."

He didn't say a word. He just stared down at her.

Mortified, Leandra hung her head, refusing to look at him. "Satisfied?" she asked in a quiet whisper.

"Not nearly enough," he replied just as quietly.

With that, he let her go, then turned to head back to the truck. Leandra followed, emerging from the shadowy garden just as the Welby children came running toward their father. She quickly shoved Nate's jacket into his hands, thinking he'd never want to kiss her again. He'd looked both shocked and appalled by her revelation.

"What were you doing in the garden?" Layla asked, suspicion in every word.

"Were you kissing?" Matt chimed in, grinning from ear to ear.

"Does this mean Miss Leandra might be my new

mommy?'' Brittney shouted as she hopped from foot to foot. ''I knew it, I just knew it.''

''Hey, hey,'' Nate said, embarrassment making his voice shaky, ''you three need to mind your own business and quit trying to rule my private life. To question number one, we were just talking. To question number two, Miss Leandra was thanking me for the birdhouse, and to question number three—Britt, Miss Leandra can't be your mother. We've talked about this, honey.''

Brittney stopped hopping and glared up at the two adults standing stiffly in front of her. ''But you said you liked her.''

Nate sighed, then ran a hand across his chin. ''I do like her.'' He turned to Leandra then. ''A lot.''

Leandra quickly quelled the relief flooding through her system. Maybe Nate wouldn't judge her as harshly as she tended to judge herself—something she realized they had in common at least—but that didn't mean he'd try kissing her again, either. She'd have to settle for being liked. A lot.

''Then what's the holdup?'' Brittney asked.

Layla moaned and turned to stare at her sister. ''The holdup, dummy, is that our daddy still loves our mama and that Miss Leandra doesn't want to be stuck with the three of us and that old, falling-down house we live in. Now, can we please go home? I've got to study for a spelling test.''

''Layla, I think you owe Miss Leandra an apology," Nate said as he stomped after his retreating daughter.

"For what?" Layla asked in defiance. "It's the truth, isn't it?" She looked from her father to Leandra, hope warring with despair in her blue eyes.

Nate lifted his head toward the stars, as if asking for God's wisdom and guidance. "I will always love your mother, no matter what happens, sunshine," he said. "And Miss Leandra will be going back to Houston after Christmas."

"So it is the truth?" Matt glanced at Leandra, his gaze accusing. "I thought you liked us, too."

Leandra didn't know how to deal with this, especially after the exchange Nate and she had just had. Bending down, she said, "Matt, I do care about all of you, but, honey, being an adult is complicated. Your father is a wonderful man, but he still misses your mother. And I don't know what I'm going to do after Christmas. But we both want what's best for all of you."

"You being my mama would be the bestest," Brittney said with a pout as she twisted a thick blond curl around her chubby finger. "Can't you please just think about it, Miss Lea?"

"It's Miss Leandra," Nate said, correcting her.

"Lea is fine," Leandra replied, turning to scoop Brittney up in her arms. "All of my friends call me Lea."

"And we are her friends," Nate told his children. "Let's just leave it at that for now, okay?"

Layla hurried to get inside the truck, slamming the door behind her. Matt gave Leandra another inquisitive look, then followed his sister. But Brittney held on to Leandra's neck and hugged her long and hard.

"I'm gonna talk to God one more time."

Leandra returned the hug, wishing with all her heart she could make this sweet child understand that she was asking too much—of both her father and Leandra.

"We can all talk to God, Brittney," she said. "Maybe He'll provide us with the answers we need."

Nate took the child from her, his eyes meeting Leandra's over Brittney's head. "Don't forget your birdhouse."

Leandra followed him to the truck, then took the bag from him, lowering her head to avoid his gaze. "Thank you. It really is beautiful."

Nate tugged at her chin so she had to look him in the eyes, his expression full of remorse and pain. "I hope it makes up for...for everything."

"It does," she said. The birdhouse made up for everything except the great pain centered in her heart. "Thank you again, Nate. Good night."

Then she turned and walked back to her own car, the memory of his kiss still as fresh as the cold wind blowing across her face.

And just as elusive.

* * *

"It's one of the most beautiful things I've ever seen," Colleen told Leandra later as they stood in the kitchen admiring the birdhouse. "And Nate made this?"

"Yes," Leandra said, her hands wrapped around the mug of hot chocolate her mother had offered her the minute she walked in the door. "Amazing, isn't it?"

"Very," Colleen said, her attention turning from the birdhouse sitting on the counter to her daughter. "What's wrong, sweetheart? Hard rehearsal tonight?"

Leandra took a long sip of the creamy liquid, marveling at her mother's ability to make it just right every time. The taste of rich chocolate milk laced with vanilla and cinnamon only made Leandra want to cry for some strange reason.

"No, rehearsal went well, actually. Everyone is getting settled into their parts and, for once, Margaret didn't make any demands. She was quite pleasant tonight for some reason."

Colleen laughed, then patted Leandra's hand. "I think Margaret's in good spirits these days because she has wonderful news to share with the rest of us."

Leandra glanced up to see the maternal pride on her mother's face. "Another baby?"

"Exactly," Colleen replied. Then she placed a finger to her lips. "But keep it quiet. She wants to announce it at Sunday dinner. You know how she likes to make a big production.'' Colleen smiled again, then tugged at Leandra's hand. ''Now tell me, what's bothering *you?*''

But Leandra's melancholy mood had just gone two shades darker. ''First Kim has another baby and now Margaret again. Those two sure are fertile.''

''They're married women,'' her mother pointed out, her eyebrows lifting. ''And most married women like to have children.''

''Not like me, I suppose,'' Leandra couldn't help but spout back. ''Single and without a maternal bone in my body, right?''

A frown skittered across her mother's face. ''I didn't mean to imply—''

''Oh, Mama, I'm sorry,'' Leandra said, pulling her mother's hands into hers. ''It's just been a long day and I guess I'm worried about the future. Christmas will be here in less than three weeks, and then my work here will be over. I don't know what to do with my life after that.''

Colleen pulled up a bar stool and indicated to Leandra to do the same. ''Are you having second thoughts about returning to Houston?''

''Yes, I think I am,'' Leandra had to admit. ''At first, I told myself I had to go back—you know, to face the music, to get back on that ol' horse. But now...'' She shrugged, tried to smile, then looked toward the window seat across the kitchen. ''I just don't know.''

Colleen looked at her daughter, her face once again as serene as always. "God has a plan for you, Lea. You know that, right?"

"Yes, I believe that with all my heart, Mama. It's just hard to sit back and wait for Him to reveal that plan. Why does He have to be so slow sometimes?"

Colleen laughed again. "Oh, you always were the impatient one. You couldn't wait to get out of Marshall and get on with your life."

Leandra nodded. "I thought my plan had been formed already. But I guess even the best laid plans change, right?"

"They sure do. And we can't blame God for that, or cast doubt about it. We just have to come up with a new plan, with His guidance."

"I'm trying," Leandra said. Then she looked down at the birdhouse. "It was so sweet of Nate to build this for us, don't you think?"

Colleen touched a hand to one of the tiny open windows on the little house. "Yes, very considerate. But then, Nathan Welby is a considerate man." Mimicking Leandra, she added, "Don't you think?"

Leandra saw the inquisitive look centered on her mother's face. "Yes, Mama. I think he's considerate, interesting, and…off-limits."

"Oh, really?"

"Really. Nate has made it very clear he's not ready for anything beyond friendship."

"Oh, and what about you?"

Leandra shook her head. "I'm not ready either. I have to get my life back on track before I can even consider having a relationship with someone again. William's betrayal left a distinct fear in my heart."

"William Myers wasn't worth your time or effort, darling. And I'm glad you got rid of him."

"More like, he got rid of me."

Colleen leaned forward. "Did you love William?"

Leandra thought about that long and hard, fighting the image of Nate's disgust when she'd told him about her past. That led to a comparison of her feelings for William with how she now felt about Nate.

But there was no comparison. The little bit of something she felt for Nate right now, this very minute, far surpassed anything she'd believed she'd felt for William.

"No, I don't think I loved him at all. I was enamored of his image, of what I thought he could do. I thought I was happy with William, and I was content to keep things on an even level, without any further commitment. I felt safe with William. There were no hassles or demands."

But all of that had changed, she remembered, the thoughts of their last days together turning her hot chocolate to a bitter taste in her mouth.

"William was exciting, dashing, wealthy, powerful. All the things I had always dreamed about in a man. But, you know, those were the very things that turned me against him in the end."

Colleen let out a long sigh. "Well, good. Because what that man expected from you could only have led to heartache and regret." Colleen got up to come around the counter. Putting a hand on each of Leandra's shoulders, she said, "You did the right thing, walking away. You stuck to your morals and the upbringing your father and I tried to instill in you. And that makes me so proud."

"Thanks, Mom," Leandra said, hugging her mother close. If only *she* could find some pride in herself again.

They both heard footsteps on the tiled floor, then parted to find Howard standing there with a questioning smile on his face. "Everything okay in here, ladies?"

"Everything is more than okay," Colleen said. "Since you both worked late tonight, I held dinner—red beans and rice."

"That sure sounds good," Howard said as he came to stand by Leandra. "I'm a starving man."

"We can't have that, now can we?" Colleen said as she took his hand across the counter.

Howard's gaze moved from his wife's face to the birdhouse. "What's this? It looks like a little Christmas cottage."

"It's a birdhouse," Colleen explained, turning it

to admire it all over again. "Nathan Welby made it for Leandra and me."

"Well, how about that." Howard whistled low, then stood back to admire the ornamental little house. Then he put a finger to his chin. "Seems to me I remember Nate and Alicia coming in to the bank a few years back to talk about this very subject."

"Birdhouses?" Leandra asked, surprised. "I got the impression this was a hobby Nate had just taken up."

"No, I'm pretty sure they wanted to talk about a possible loan—to start some sort of craft business. Alicia went on and on about how Nate could create anything from wood."

Leandra looked down at the lovely house. So, Alicia had been in on this dream, this design, too. Somehow, that rubbed salt in her already wounded heart. She'd believed Nate had created this just for her.

Turning back to her father, she asked, "What happened? Why didn't they start the business?"

"She died a little while after that, honey. Guess Nate didn't have the heart after that." He went to the refrigerator to take out the tea pitcher. "I was prepared to give them the loan, too. It would have been risky, but they seemed so excited and happy.... Of course, you are not to repeat that, understand?"

Leandra nodded absently, then sat still as her father's voice trailed off. So Nate had had a dream of creating these beautiful houses, of turning it into a business. And yet, that dream had crashed right along with his wife's plane.

Dead. Put aside in a cloud of grief.

Until now.

Suddenly, her heart soared with renewed hope. Regardless of Alicia's influence, Nate had designed this house for her, for her family.

For Leandra.

Maybe he was beginning to work through his grief. Maybe he did feel something besides friendship for her, after all.

And maybe there was a way she could show him that she supported him and believed in him.

A lot.

Chapter Eight

"Daddy's not home yet," Layla told Leandra two days later.

Leandra stood on the porch of the big house with Mutt sniffing at her long trouser skirt. She wondered why she'd acted on impulse and decided to ride out to the Welby place. She had tons of extra work to do—Chet thought she'd make a great marketing director for the city—and apparently in his mind, had already hired her for the job.

Standing here now, she thought burying herself in work would be the perfect solution to keeping her mind off Nate Welby and his children. And yet, here she was at their front door.

"Well, can I come in anyway?" Leandra asked, hoping she could at least have a talk with Layla while she was here. The girl was obviously in need of some feminine attention, but all that attitude got in the way.

"I don't know—"

Before Layla could finish the sentence, Brittney came bouncing down the stairs. "Miss Lea! I'm so glad you're here. We need help with the Christmas decorations."

Layla gave her young sister a warning look. "Dad said we have to wait until he gets home, remember."

Brittney shook her head, causing her two long pigtails to swing from side to side over her shoulders. "Uh-uh. He said we needed adult superfision."

"Adult super*vision,* squirt," Layla corrected. "And you need a speech therapist."

"Do not.

"Do, too."

"Girls, girls," Leandra said, still waiting on the porch, still petting the overly friendly dog, "please don't fight. I'd be glad to help, as long as Layla thinks it's okay for me to come inside."

Layla looked back at Leandra, her expression changing from concerned to resigned. "Well, you aren't a stranger and you are an adult. Yeah, sure. I guess Daddy won't mind. He's working late *as usual.*"

She backed up to open the big door wide. Mutt took that as his cue to come in. He pranced ahead of Leandra and headed up the wide wooden staircase, barking, his shaggy tail wagging. She heard Matt calling out to the dog upstairs.

Leandra stepped into the foyer, her eyes scanning the large, spacious rooms. "Wow, this place is incredible. It's so big and airy."

"And drafty," Layla said, pulling her zippered fleece jacket tighter around her midsection as she looked longingly at the empty fireplace. "We aren't allowed to start a fire when Daddy's not here. He's worked on the furnace, but sometimes it still goes out. We're supposed to get a new one after Christmas."

Brittney nodded, then took Leandra by the hand. "Yeah, cause Daddy's getting a big bonus check from his boss. That's how he's gonna fix the furnace. And we get presents, too."

"That's good," Leandra replied as she allowed the child to guide her into what looked like the den off to the right. On the left, a matching room held a huge battered antique dining table and eight matching chairs.

"Twin parlors," Leandra said, marveling at the potential of the house. "That dining table is beautiful."

"My mama bought it at a garage sale," Layla said. "She'd planned on redoing it, but..."

Her voice trailed off, causing Leandra to glance over at her. "Your mother sounds like a wonderful person."

"That's her picture," Brittney said, pointing to a brass-framed print over the fireplace mantel.

Leandra didn't have to see a picture of Alicia Welby to know the woman was perfect in every way. Long blond hair, big blue eyes, a smile that would light up any summer meadow. She could just imagine Nate and Alicia, running through a field of wildflowers together, falling down in the grass, laughing, loving.

Shaking away the image, Leandra decided she'd made a big mistake, coming out here. She wanted to see the rest of Nate's designs, talk to him about producing them for the public. But now, she wasn't so sure Nate would be ready for that.

But she'd already talked to Richard about the possibility of Nate displaying some of his birdhouses in Richard's store out on the highway. Flanagan's Food and General Merchandise would be the perfect place to showcase Nate's work, since the store was designed like an old-fashioned general store and carried art and crafts by several local artisans.

Once Richard had seen the house Nate had made, he agreed Nate had talent and could probably sell lots of the dainty little birdhouses. Especially during Christmas. It made perfect sense to Leandra.

But would it make sense to Nate?

Well, all she could do was ask. If he said no, then that would be that.

In the meantime, she could at least spend some

time with his children and help them get this lovely old house ready for the Christmas season. That would save Nate some time and maybe improve his own spirits.

And she'd start by building a fire in the fireplace.

He couldn't make any sense of the way he'd been feeling lately.

Nate turned the pickup off the interstate, taking the highway that would lead him home. Just ahead, the sun was setting over the western sky, and with it that old sense of dread settled around Nate's shoulders like a welcome yoke.

He always dreaded going home. He loved his children, but pulling the truck up that long gravel driveway every night was one of the hardest things he had to do.

Until now.

Lately, Nate hadn't been dreading it as much as he used to. And that had him confused and wondering, and even more determined than ever to hang on to his dread.

If he let go of the dread, of the pain, then he would be dishonoring his wife's memory, wouldn't he?

If he thought about kissing Leandra Flanagan again, as he'd done just about every waking hour over the past couple of days, then he'd be unfaithful to Alicia, wouldn't he?

"Tell me, Lord," he said out loud, beating a

hand against the steering wheel. "Tell me how to let go—of both of them."

He longed to be free of the guilt and grief that had colored his world for so long, longed to let go and give his children the love and attention he knew they craved. But if he gave in to this need to be free, that would mean having to finally let go of Alicia, too.

And he wasn't ready to do that.

And yet, Leandra's kiss kept beckoning him.

Her lips had been so soft, so sweet against his. That sweetness had jolted him all the way to his toes.

Which was why nothing made any sense anymore. How could he have feelings for two completely different women—one dead, one very much alive?

His dread was being replaced with a new feeling, one that he really wasn't ready to acknowledge.

And yet it was there, staring him in the face, coloring his melancholy with vivid shades of autumn fire. Liquid brown eyes, flashing. Fiery brunette hair, shining in the sun. A bright smile that seemed to change even the worst winter day to something bright and brilliant. And a big heart, so big it seemed to be trying to burst out of her petite little body.

Leandra.

He didn't want to hope. Couldn't bring himself

to put a name to his feelings. He wanted to cling like a desperate, drowning man to his only lifeline.

His dead wife.

One more mile and he'd be home.

Then a voice echoed through the rumbling truck, a voice so clear, so distinct, that Nate thought he'd left the radio on.

But it wasn't the radio.

Alicia's not coming back, Nate. She's gone and she's at peace now. She'd want you to find your own peace. She'd want you to love again.

"No," Nate said, fighting against what he already knew in his heart. "No, I'm not ready yet."

And then he turned the truck off the road, toward his home. And slammed on the brakes so hard, gravel spewed up to hit the driver's side door.

Dusk surrounded the old white house. Dusk, and a thousand twinkling white lights strung around the porch posts, and across the front of the gabled roof. White icicle lights that moved and glittered like golden-white stars.

And on the door, a big evergreen wreath with a red and gold shiny ribbon trailing down from its top.

Somebody had decorated his house for the holidays.

Somebody had dared to disrupt Alicia's memory, her domain, *his* sacred, sad sanctuary.

And he had a pretty good idea just who that somebody was.

The little whisper of hope was gone now. And the dread was back, a welcome ally as Nate prepared to do battle.

"She might be gone," he told the voice he'd heard earlier, "but that doesn't mean I'm ready to have someone come in and take over completely."

It was time he got his head back on straight, then set Leandra Flanagan straight about a few things.

Nate entered the house, ready to roar his outrage. But he stopped just inside the door, his roar turning to a whimper of protest that he couldn't begin to voice.

There was a fire in the fireplace.

The mantel had been decorated with red, glowing candles and magnolia leaves. The den had been cleaned up, the pillows fluffed, the throw rugs straightened and swept. Two bright, fresh poinsettias sat on either side of the huge hearth.

He had to shut his eyes to the sheer beauty of it.

Hearing laughter in the kitchen, he opened his eyes and turned to the big dining room that they never used. It was set for dinner, with the old, chipped china they'd bought secondhand years ago. Another poinsettia graced the center of the table, and on the mismatched buffet, white candles burned in the silver candelabras Alicia had found at a flea market.

Everything looked homey and cozy, like a scene

from a spread in a magazine. Everything seemed perfect.

Except for the horrible smell coming from the kitchen.

Determined to nip this intrusion in the bud, Nate stomped down the hallway to the rear of the house, intent on giving Miss Leandra Flanagan a dressing down she would never forget.

Instead, he came upon a scene he would always remember.

His three children were centered around the butcher block counter he'd build years ago, flour on their hands and all over their faces, their backs to him as they watched Leandra and noisily offered encouraging instructions. Mutt lay by the back door, a dubious expression coloring his dark eyes. When the dog saw Nate, he lifted his head, rolled his doggy eyes, as if to say, "Don't ask," then whimpered and flopped his head down on his paws to stare up at his master.

But the woman standing by the stove really caught Nate's attention. Leandra had more flour all over her than any of the kids. It was in her hair, on her hands, all over her black cashmere sweater, and all the way down her checked trouser skirt. She even had flour dusted across her black loafers.

"What's going on around here?"

At the sound of his voice, the room went silent. Nate's children and Leandra all whirled around at the same time.

"Daddy, you're home!" Brittney said, rushing to fling herself in his arms. "Did you see? Did you see the lights? We did it ourselves. Miss Leandra wouldn't let me get up on the ladder, though. I got to do the short parts."

"I saw, pumpkin," Nate said, giving the child a kiss before he set her down and wiped a dab of flour from his own face. He glanced toward Leandra then. "I've seen all of it. You've been very busy."

Matt pointed at the stove. "And we're making you chicken and dumplings for supper."

Layla shrugged, then wiped her hands down the front of her jeans. "Except, we sorta burned the first batch."

"That explains the smell, at least," Nate replied, his gaze still locked with Leandra's. "I thought I told you kids, no cooking or fires while I'm not here."

"But Miss Leandra's an adult," Brittney pointed out.

"Are you sure about that?" Nate said, then instantly regretted it when he saw the hurt look in her dark eyes.

"I'm sorry," she said at last. "I can't cook. But I wanted—"

"She wanted to make you dinner," Brittney interjected, "and surprise you with the decorations. And tomorrow, we're going to get a tree, right, Miss Leandra?"

"If your father doesn't object," Leandra said, her hurt expression hidden by a slight smile. "Now, I'd better watch this new batch of dumplings. Maybe this time, I'll get it right."

Matt glanced over into the bubbling pot of white mush. "Yeah, cause Mutt wouldn't even eat the last batch and that dog eats anything."

Upon hearing his name, Mutt lifted his head, sniffed, then got up and ran from the room, his tail wagging a hasty farewell.

Leandra's smile turned into a frown. "I *can't* cook. I don't know why I tried. I shouldn't have done this."

Layla shot Nate a warning look, then hurried to the stove. "But these dumplings look okay, Miss Leandra. Really. And they smell good, too."

"Better than the last ones," Matt said, grinning.

Brittney pulled Nate close, tugging at his hand. "See, Daddy, don't them look right?"

"It's those," Layla corrected.

"Okay, okay," Brittney said, moaning. Then she made a dramatic effort to correct herself. "*Those* dumplings look just right."

Some of Nate's initial anger drained away, to be replaced with a teasing tone. "Well, how many poor chickens had to die for this dinner?"

"Only one," Layla told him. "We used canned broth with the chicken broth to make the dumplings, but we got most of the chicken out before the dumplings got scorched. We had more canned broth, so we started another pot with that.''

"I'm going to drop the chicken meat in once I see if this batch is edible," Leandra told him. "Honestly, I don't know what went wrong. This is my mother's recipe and I followed her instructions."

Nate stared over at her, enjoying the skittish way she tried to explain, her hands lifting in the air with each word. Which only made little flour dust balls float out all around her. Then he reminded himself that he was supposed to be angry with her.

"We just forgot to turn the heat down," Matt explained, wiping even more flour across his smudged face.

Leandra checked the burner button, then went to the sink to wash her hands. "Hopefully, this will be ready in about ten minutes." Then she turned to the children. "Let's get this cleaned up, and we'll get the salad and tea out of the refrigerator. I'll drop the chicken back in to heat it up, and Matt, you can pour the milk."

The three children went to work wiping down the flour-dusted counter while Leandra tried to dust herself off with a dish towel.

After the children had gone into the dining room, carrying drinks and condiments for the salad, Nate walked over to Leandra. "Why'd you do all of this?"

She looked up then, into his eyes. With a little

shrug, she said, "I'm wondering that same thing myself." Lowering her head, she added, "You're mad."

Nate couldn't deny that. "I *was* good and mad, yeah. When I pulled up and saw all those lights—"

"The children asked me to help, Nate." She gazed up at him then, a pleading look centered in her eyes. "I came by to see you, but you weren't home yet. They wanted to decorate, so I agreed to help. Then we had so much fun, and you were late, and it was dinnertime and they told me you like dumplings—" She stopped, turned back to the sink. "I'm sorry."

Nate tried to find the words he needed to say. He wanted to tell her that this wasn't her house, that she had no right to just come barreling in here and take over, changing things around, trying to make this house something it could never be.

But when she looked up at him, with flour smudged across her cheek, with her heart in her eyes, all he could do was reach out and touch her face. "You've got a glob of flour right there," he said, his fingers brushing away the white specks. Then he smiled. "Actually, you've got flour on just about every part of you."

Leandra let out a little rush of breath. "I think I've got more on me and the kitchen floor than in the dumplings," she said. "We should have just ordered pizza."

"They don't deliver way out here," he replied,

his fingers still touching on her face. "And I do like dumplings, even scorched ones."

She reached up to take his hand away. "But you're angry with me. I—I overstepped the bounds, didn't I?"

"Yes, you did," he admitted. "We normally don't go all out for Christmas."

"But why not?"

"It just makes...it makes it harder."

"But the children—"

"My children are just fine. They've been just fine."

"So you *are* angry, and you think I should mind my own business?"

"Something like that."

She pushed past him then. Taking the plate of chopped chicken off the counter, she dumped it into the dumpling pot, stirred it, then turned off the burner. "Well, here's your dinner. And I'll be leaving now."

"Hey, wait just a minute," Nate said, reaching out to catch her by the hand. "Since you cooked it, you have to eat it. Or are you afraid you'll get food poisoning?"

"Don't try to make me feel better, Nate. I messed up and now I don't know how to fix it."

"More flour and a new pot," he replied, his hand in hers. "Don't leave."

"But, I'm so stupid. I thought—"

"You wanted to help my children," he reminded

her. "Look, Leandra, I know how persuasive those three can be, especially when they gang up on a person. And they know that you're too nice to turn them down."

She looked down at the floor. "It was hard to say no, but I enjoyed helping them decorate. They said you hadn't done it in a long time."

"No, and I did promise them," he said, guilt in each word. "It's just hard sometimes."

She glanced back up then, her eyes wide. "But it can get easier, Nate. With time and prayer. That's what my mother always tells me when I'm struggling with a big problem."

"Time and prayer," he repeated. "Seems like I'm all out of both."

"You only have to ask."

He let go of her hand then. "Ask what—that God give me my wife back, that He show me how to give my children the life they deserve? What should I ask for, Leandra?"

"You're mad again."

"I've been mad for the last three years," he retorted, pushing a hand through his hair in frustration.

"Then you need to ask for relief, Nate. You need to find some peace, some closure." She reached a hand to his face, her fingers treading like an angel's wings over his skin. "You need to let go of the past and look toward the future."

The need he felt for her then caused him to back

away. He couldn't, wouldn't pull her into his arms and ask God for salvation or peace. He would fight against this, with his every breath. Because he liked being miserable too much.

"I'm not ready to let go," he told her.

"I know," Leandra replied. "And that's why I should just leave right now."

But she didn't get to leave, after all. Brittney bounced into the room, pushing between them. "Can we eat? I'm starving."

Nate picked up his daughter, then tickled her tummy, his smile belying the darkness in his eyes. "I'm hungry myself. And I sure don't want to miss out on those dumplings." Looking at Leandra over Brittney's head, he said, "C'mon, Leandra. You cooked. You get to serve. And then, I'll wash the dishes and clear up everything else."

"Not everything, Nate," Leandra told him as she whirled past him. "There's a lot that needs to be cleared up between us, but I don't think you're ready to admit that just yet."

Chapter Nine

Nate had cleaned the kitchen, all right. After they'd eaten dinner, with the children laughing and talking over the loud silence between the two adults, he'd promptly done his part, then stomped off to the barn to "check on Honeyboy and do some work." That left Leandra with the children. Since tomorrow was Saturday, she'd told them to settle into their pajamas so they could watch a late movie.

Earlier, in the midst of a fit of impulsiveness, she'd promised them hot chocolate and cookies by the fire, to cap off what she had hoped would be a lovely evening. But that had backfired the minute their father had arrived, with a pop every bit as loud as the dry wood now crackling in the fireplace.

Nate did not appreciate any of her efforts.

And to think she'd started out with the best of intentions.

Since they'd had the night off from rehearsals, she'd decided it would be a good time to talk to Nate about mass marketing his birdhouses. Then, suddenly, she'd been up on a ladder stringing Christmas lights—lights that she'd had her brother Richard deliver from his store, along with the poinsettias and candles, and supplies for making dumplings.

"You're turning into a domestic dynamo," Richard had teased on the phone. "What else did you need? A chicken and three cans of chicken broth? Leandra, I'm worried about you—if you're cooking for this man, that means it's serious, and that also means his health is in serious danger."

Although her brother had been joking, his words now rang true. She'd not only ruined dinner, but also any chances of furthering things with Nate.

And since when had she decided to further things, anyway? Since that kiss, dummy, she told herself as she poured hot chocolate into mugs on a big tray next to the cookies. She then carried it into the den where the kids sat already watching the movie.

Seeing the three Welby children all curled up with pillows and blankets by the roaring fire only added to Leandra's misery. She wanted Nate there, too. She wanted to curl up with him by that fire.

But Nate had retreated into his memories and his guilt.

"Does your father work in the barn every night?" she asked Layla now, concern for the girl motivating her question.

"Just about," Layla replied as she took a mug from Leandra. "He's always taking on extra work, even though he's been promoted at his regular job."

"But surely he spends time with you, right?"

"Only when he's forced to," Layla said, her words low so the younger children wouldn't hear. Then she added, "He's a good daddy, Miss Lea. He just misses our mama, and I guess you figured out I look just like her."

Leandra nodded. "You're just as pretty."

"That's why he hates me," Layla blurted out. Then, clearly mortified, she said, "Don't tell him I said that."

Leandra put her cocoa down on a nearby table. "Honey, you're wrong. Your father loves you. Surely you know that."

"He loves me because he has to—that's his duty as a father. But..." Her voice trailed off, and Leandra watched her swallow back the tears. "I remind him of her and because of that, he hates being around me. That's why he goes out to that old barn every night."

"Oh, baby." Leandra pulled the girl into her

arms, rocking her back and forth while silent tears slipped down Layla's face. "Shh. Don't cry now."

"What's the matter?" Brittney asked, ever curious even if she was sleepy-eyed.

"The movie," Leandra said, grabbing the first excuse she could find. "This is the sad part and Layla doesn't want to watch. Better hurry, or you'll miss the ending."

With that, Brittney snuggled back down inside her old quilt. "Don't be sad, sister. It's just a movie."

Leandra wished life could be that way—just like a movie or a book with a happy ending. But life didn't always play out the way people dreamed it would.

"Have you talked to your father about this?" she asked Layla a while later, after the girl had settled down and both Brittney and Matt were snoozing on the floor by the fire.

Pushing Leandra away, Layla fought for the attitude that had kept her true emotions hidden so well. "He's not the talking kind, or haven't you noticed?"

"Yes, I've noticed," Leandra admitted. "But if you went to him, told him how this makes you feel—"

"No," Layla said, jumping up off the couch. "I couldn't do that. He'd just get even more mad at me. He doesn't like to talk about Mama at all. And Brittney is always asking questions—she was too young to even remember Mama. It would just make things worse if he knew I'd said something to you.'' Grabbing her blanket, she said, ''You can't say anything, Miss Lea, please. You can't tell him.''

''I won't, I promise,'' Leandra told the jittery teen. ''But he needs to know, honey.''

''He knows,'' Layla said, the wisdom of the two words warring with her youthful expression.

Suddenly, Leandra understood the girl's predicament. Layla and Nate were tiptoeing around each other, each trying hard not to disturb Alicia's memories. And neither of them had even come close to dealing with her death.

That had been obvious tonight.

Nate had been so angry! She'd seen it, felt it, the minute he'd entered the kitchen. And just because his children had wanted the house decorated. But he didn't want anything changed or rearranged. He wanted to keep this house intact, even though it was in obvious need of some tender loving care. He wanted to freeze time, to keep things the way they were when Alicia had lived in this house.

''Well, she wouldn't want this,'' Leandra told herself a few minutes later as she rinsed their cups and put away the cookies. ''She would want her children to be happy and healthy. She'd want them to celebrate life, not preserve it in a time warp. And she'd want you to be happy, too, Nate.''

But would she want you to be with someone like me?

Leandra finally got the children off to bed, then turned to go out to the barn. "I'm going to tell him I'm leaving now," she said to Mutt. "And while I'm at it, I just might give the man a piece of my mind, too."

Mutt whimpered his response to that suggestion, then wagged his tail in anticipation.

Nate moved the tiny piece of wood back and forth through his fingers, trying to decide if he wanted to carve it into a leaf or a flower.

Then again, maybe he'd just leave it the way it was. Why couldn't people leave well enough alone, anyway?

He thought of Leandra, standing in the middle of his kitchen, standing in the very spot where Alicia had stood so many nights. He could still hear Leandra's laughter as he'd entered the front door tonight.

But he couldn't remember Alicia's laugh.

And that hurt so much.

Throwing the wood down, Nate stood there staring at his workbench. He couldn't even hide behind his work tonight. Couldn't even think beyond Leandra trying to make dumplings.

Dumplings!

He'd eaten them, scorched parts and all, just to please his children, just to be polite to her, and actually, the food hadn't been half bad. And all the while, he'd noticed her hair, shining softly in the candlelight, her laughter echoing across the table at him, calling out to him, her eyes, beseeching and encouraging, glancing his way as she chattered away with his children.

Her lips.

"How can I feel this way, Lord? How can I want to be with another woman? A completely different woman?"

Different in so many ways.

Yet, so like his Alicia in other ways.

Leandra had once again been kind to his children. She'd once again taken over where no one else had bothered to even lend a hand. She'd put their needs, their requests, above her own comfort. She'd made them happy, laughing and carefree again.

And that, he had to admit, had been her saving grace.

Suddenly, all the anger drained out of Nate, leaving him with a fatigue so great, he swayed against the sturdy workbench. "I need some help here, God."

"You sure do," Leandra said from the open doorway.

Nate whirled to find her standing there, staring at him, her hands in the big pockets of her wool overcoat. He didn't miss the pain etched across her face. He could see it clearly from the dim overhead light.

"Go ahead," she said as she walked closer. "Tell Him your troubles. Don't let me interfere."

Nate shuffled his feet, looked down at the sawdust covered floor. "Can't a man have a private moment to pray around here, at least?"

"I'm sorry," Leandra said, backing out of the barn. "I just wanted you to know the children are in bed and I'm going home."

"Wait," he said, turning around. "We need to talk about a few things. You said we needed to clear the air."

Leandra stopped just outside the door. "I came out here to do that very thing, but now I think the air is completely clear, and so are your feelings toward me and my…intrusion. Again, I am so sorry."

Nate let out an irritated sigh, then in two long strides had her by the arm, pulling her back inside the barn. "Would you just quit apologizing? You haven't done anything wrong."

She scoffed, glanced away. "Oh, except decorate a house you didn't want to decorate in the first place, no matter what you promised your children. Except cook a meal that turned out to be a fiasco even on the second try, and make myself a general all-around nuisance. I'd say that's a lot to be sorry about."

Nate stared down at her, hoping to make her understand everything that was troubling his tired heart.

"It's not you," he told her, his hands on her arms. "It's me, Leandra. It's my bad attitude, my problems, me and my pain and guilt, and my lack of faith."

"Oh, I understand," she told him, her eyes glistening in a pool of unshed tears. "And that's why I came to say good-night. I won't push myself off on you again, Nate. It was foolish, considering that I've already been through one bad relationship. I should have learned from that, but no, I had to come home, take on this job just to tell myself I'm still worthy of some kind of work, then just like that, I saw you standing by that pasture, with your dog and your horse and your three adorable children, and I got this funny notion all the way down to my toes."

"Leandra—"

"No," she said, pushing him away as she turned her back to him. "I guess I was on the rebound, you know. Same old tired reasoning. I took all the signals the wrong way, wanted more from you than you were willing to give. But, I can see it all so plainly now. You don't want my help, don't need me in your life. You've got it all planned out, exactly the way you want it."

She whirled then. "Except that your children are suffering because you are so lost in the past, you can't even begin to see that they need their father."

"I'm a good father," he said, anger clouding his better judgment.

"Yes, you are," she replied. "You are a good, dutiful father. You do all the things that are expected of you. But what about the unexpected, Nate? What about that?"

The anger was back, refreshing and nurturing, and so welcome he almost cried out with relief. "You have no right to come into my home like this and tell me how to raise my children. You don't know the first thing about children, and from everything I've seen, you don't even want to have any of your own."

She stood there in the moonlight, her hands shoved in the pockets of her coat, shivering. Silent. But her eyes, oh, he'd never forget the pain in her eyes. That pain shouted a message, a warning, to him.

He wanted to take back what he'd just said, but the words were still echoing out over the night. Never to be taken back.

"Leandra," he said, reaching for her.

"No," she said again, her voice strained and husky. "You're absolutely right, Nate. I don't know anything about raising children. I never thought I'd want children. I thought I had my life all mapped out and then everything changed. Everything turned ugly and I came home, a complete and utter failure."

She shrugged, her laughter brittle with a bitterness that tore through his hard heart and made his anger feel like a brick pressing against his windpipe. "I guess you and the children were just a distraction, a way to prove to myself that I had a heart, and some maternal qualities, after all. But, hey, I even failed at that, too, didn't I?"

He tried to reach out to her again, and again, she pushed him away, her hand flying out in defense.

"No, it's all right. I understand what you're trying to say to me. We weren't meant for each other, and it's silly and a waste of time for us to pretend. So...let's just keep this as business. You're just about finished with the set and the props and I've got your check all ready down at city hall. Two more weeks and I'll be on my way back to Houston." She whirled and started toward her car. "And then, I guess I'll see what else I can do to make my life a total mess."

Nathan stood there, stunned, as she got in her car and backed it around. And then she was gone, leaving him to stare off into the night.

Mutt came running up, whimpering for attention. But Nate couldn't give the dog the attention he craved.

Maybe Leandra was right, he thought as he locked up the barn and made his way to the house. Maybe he was making all the right moves, but would he ever be able to really love anyone again?

Would he ever be able to give his children the one thing they needed the most—his heart?

That heart hurt tonight, hurt from the cold wind on his back, from the cruel words he'd flung out at Leandra, and mostly, it hurt from her response, her own self-condemning speech.

He'd caused her pain, the one thing he'd hoped

to avoid. He'd turned things around, blamed her for his own inconsistencies, his own failures.

"I shouldn't have let things go this far," he reasoned as Mutt hit the porch ahead of him. "I shouldn't have flirted with her, teased her. And I surely shouldn't have kissed her there in the prayer garden."

But you did, Nate. Now what are you gonna do about it?

"Mutt, did you learn how to speak?" Nate asked, glancing around.

But Nate knew that what he'd just heard had come somewhere from deep inside himself. His conscience was arguing with him.

His conscience was telling him to go after Leandra and ask her for another chance.

"I'm not going to listen, not tonight," he said out loud. "I've already hurt her enough."

Mutt groaned, then barked to be let inside where it was warm, where his bed waited just inside the pantry doorway.

"I hear you, boy," Nate told the dog. "It's gonna be a long, cold night, that's for sure."

Especially with the scent of Leandra's perfume, and a faint whiff of scorched dumplings, still lingering in his mind.

Chapter Ten

The next Monday night was hard for Leandra. They would rehearse early in the afternoon and on some nights this week, to accommodate everyone's work schedules. Now that the children were out of school for the holidays, everyone was more able to go through a full-scale dress rehearsal. Soon though, it would be the real thing in front of a sold-out audience each night.

Next week, the pageant would have a four-day run with the last performance ending on Christmas Eve, just before the annual candlelight service at the church across the street. The service was every bit as popular and anticipated as the pageant. Leandra expected a big crowd there, too.

Now that the pageant was becoming a reality, it seemed almost anticlimactic. She should be excited. The rehearsals were going well. The stage decorations and props were incredible, and everything was moving along right on schedule. She'd worked so hard, such long hours, not only on the pageant but on several other projects Chet had dropped in her lap, and becoming involved with Nate and his children had only added to both the stress and the joy of this whole production. What would she do once this was all over?

Things were already over, she told herself. At least as far as Nate was concerned.

All weekend, she'd dreaded tonight, dreaded seeing Nate's face, the memory of his words forever etched in her being as a reminder of her utter failure.

"You don't know the first thing about raising children. You don't even want children."

He had been so right. And so wrong.

Because she'd changed over the past few weeks.

Now, Leandra's heart was playing tricks on her. Now, each time she thought about being in that drafty old house with the three Welby children, drinking hot chocolate and eating cookies by the fire, she only longed to have that chance again. Over and over again.

All day Saturday, she'd moped around until her mother had put her to work wrapping Christmas gifts. Sunday, she'd gone to church, hoping to find some solace in Reverend Powell's powerful words. But even the scriptures leading up to the birth of Jesus couldn't bring her any joy.

Sunday afternoon, she'd gone for a long walk in the cold, praying, listening, hoping to find some answers in her silent meditations.

But now, as she sat here watching people file in for the rehearsal, she knew there was only one answer.

She couldn't fall in love with Nathan Welby.

She wouldn't fall in love with Nathan Welby.

She'd certainly never set out to do that.

Quickly, she made a mental inventory of why she'd been thrown into this situation in the first place.

I quit my job. I came home. Wanted to stay busy, so took job as pageant coordinator. Had to hire a carpenter. Children wanted me to be their mommy. Couldn't do that, so decided to be a good friend, even though I'm terribly attracted to their daddy.

It should have ended there, except that she'd rushed headlong into asking Nate and the children to Thanksgiving dinner.

That dinner, at least, had been nice. Wonderful, except that her mother's vase had been broken.

Nate gave me a birdhouse. *For my mother.*

Nate kissed me.

I got this crazy notion to help him sell birdhouses. So I went out to house. Got talked into building a fire, decorating for Christmas, and cooking dinner. Ruined dinner. Ruined our friendship. Ruined everything.

Fools rush in where angels fear to tread.

And now I am utterly confused and miserable.

End of list. End of story.

Now, she had to muster up the courage to face him. She didn't have any choice. She had to get through this week, then the performances next week, and then it would be over.

"I can do that," she said out loud. "I have to finish what I started."

"You're talking to yourself," Margaret told her as she sat down in the seat beside Leandra. Then she took one look at Leandra's face and groaned.

"My, what's wrong with you? Are you coming down with the flu? I don't want the baby exposed—"

Leandra took Margaret's hand away from her stomach. "I don't have the flu, so stop worrying. I'm just in a mood. Tired, I guess."

Margaret grinned knowingly then poked Leandra on the arm with a slim finger, her diamond solitaire shining in the muted auditorium light. "Richard told Jack and me about your dinner with the Welbys. No wonder you're exhausted. Cooking for those three children and that man—"

"I'd rather not talk about that," Leandra said, her tone dismissive. "And Richard shouldn't have told you, either."

Margaret twisted around to stare at her. "Oh, he just thought it was so sweet. Face it, Leandra, you've never gone to this much trouble for a man before. We're all dying to hear the details."

Leandra got up, her clipboard and papers clutched to her chest. "Look, there are no details." Then glaring down at the dubious expression on Margaret's face, she added, "And just for the record, I *did* cook for William every now and then."

"But mostly, according to what little you've told me about the time you spent with William, you ate just about every meal out," Margaret interjected. "You told me that. Told me he took you to fancy restaurants all over Houston."

"Well, that's over and so is any more attempts to cook for the Welbys," Leandra said, her patience snapping.

Margaret got up, too, then placed a hand on Leandra's arm, the teasing lilt in her voice gone. "Are you okay?"

Leandra saw the concern in her sister-in-law's eyes, and instantly regretted her outburst. "I'm fine, Margaret. Just stressed about this production. I'm sorry I took it out on you."

Margaret patted her arm. "You know you can tell me anything, and I won't blab like Richard did. Not if you really don't want me to—just say so."

"Thanks," Leandra told her, appreciative of Margaret's rare show of discretion. She felt sure she *could* trust Margaret if she really needed to confide in her, but Leandra wasn't ready for that. "It's nothing, honestly. I just overstepped my place with Nathan and now I feel awful about it. I shouldn't have cooked dinner at all. And I intend to keep my distance from now on.'' Then she glanced around and whispered low, ''He's not over Alicia.''

Understanding colored Margaret's big eyes. ''Oh, I see. You know, Lea, it's hard to lose someone we love. Friends and family try to bring us comfort, but it takes a long time to accept. Death is so final, and the answers aren't easy. Maybe Nate's just not ready to take that next step.'' She shrugged then shook her head. ''And…I'd sure be hesitant about stepping in to fill Alicia's shoes. How she put up with those children—''

Leandra held out a hand to quiet her, almost glad Margaret had stopped philosophizing and was now back to her old snobbish self. ''I know. But believe me, the children aren't the problem. I've figured it all out in my head. I was on the rebound from breaking up with William. I needed to feel needed, and the children pulled me into this relationship. Nate is a kind, wonderful man, but I'm pulling myself out. As of now.''

''Oh, really?'' Margaret sounded doubtful. ''Well, I hope for your sake, that's true.'' She placed her hands on Leandra's shoulder, then leaned close. '''Cause Nate and the children just walked through the back door.''

He tried not to look for her. But Nate couldn't help himself. His gaze automatically searched the crowd gathered in the auditorium, looking for Leandra.

Then he saw her, standing on the other side near the stage with her back to him, talking to Margaret.

This was going to be hard.

All weekend, he'd cursed himself for a fool. He shouldn't have treated her so callously after she'd been so nice and helpful to his children.

His children, he reminded himself now. Leandra had tried to tell him how to take care of his own children. That wasn't right.

But she'd been right about him. And so very wrong, too.

He loved his children. Yet he knew he'd been avoiding them, letting them drift along on the coattails of that love. He'd only been mad because Leandra had pointed out the obvious. Yet, he wasn't ready to let someone else in on his misery. He wasn't ready to relinquish paternal rights to another woman besides their mother.

He'd just have to do better at being their father. Having thought about this all weekend, he'd made good on his promise by taking the children to a movie, then Christmas shopping. He'd even toyed with the idea of taking them to church on Sunday, but a million excuses clouded that promise right out of the way. He had stayed away from the barn, at least. They'd put up a Christmas tree on Sunday afternoon.

And he could still remember Brittney's words.

"I thought Miss Lea was going to help us decorate the tree, Daddy."

"She couldn't make it, honeypie. But we'll get the job done."

And he would get the job done. Alone. He didn't need some city woman telling him how to raise his children, how to decorate his house, how to...smile again, laugh again, feel again.

He didn't need Leandra Flanagan.

So here he stood, trying hard to be a good father, trying hard to live up to the pressure, the pain, hoping he could make it through this next week of staying here in the same room with her to watch his children rehearse. He'd promised them he wouldn't leave. He was going to keep that promise, no matter how much he wanted to go to Leandra and beg her to come back and make more dumplings.

"We have a major problem," Chet Reynolds told Leandra a few minutes later.

Everyone was settled into the seats directly below the stage to go over last minute business items. Leandra intended to make a few suggestions when Chet came rushing in the back door, his hands waving, his big feet flapping against the concrete floor.

"What's the matter, Chet?" she asked, concerned for the man's health. His face was red and he was breathing heavy from rushing up the aisle.

"It's the lion," Chet began, then took a long calming breath, his Adam's apple bobbing. "And the lamb."

Leandra glanced around. "Where is Mr. Emory

anyway? He's our lion and he gets to try on his costume tonight.''

"Was our lion," Chet said, waving his hands again. "He had a heart attack about two hours ago. He's in the hospital."

"Oh, my." Leandra hated hearing bad news such as this. Mr. Emory was a sweet old man and he loved being a part of the theater since he'd done some acting in his younger days. He wouldn't want to miss out on being the lion in this production. "I hope he's going to be all right," she said above the murmur of concern moving through the crowd.

"He's fine," Chet told her, his sentences choppy and breathless. "Lucky it was mild. Rest and therapy. But he can't be in the pageant. Doctor's orders."

"I understand," Leandra said. "And I sure hope Mr. Emory recovers soon. Luckily, we still have time to find another lion. Someone tall and willing to roar a bit now and then."

"My Daddy'd be perfect for that," Matt shouted, grinning from ear to ear. "He roars at us all the time."

Leandra's gaze instantly connected with Nate's. He was sitting at the back of the crowd, slightly away from the main players. After hearing Matt's rather loud suggestion, Nate slouched down in his seat and ran a hand over his chin in agitation.

Before Leandra could say anything, Chet spoke

up. "Nate, you would make a good lion. You got the right coloring and everything."

Nate stood up, then shook his head. "Nah. I'm only here to help with the set. I work behind the scenes."

"But Daddy, we need you," Layla said, twisting in her seat to stare at her father. "We don't have much time and all you have to do is march out when we're singing the animal song."

"And he gets to roar really loud," Matt reminded her.

After the laughter had settled down, Nate stood there with his hands in the pockets of his jeans, a distressed look covering his face. "Oh, all right," he said at last, defeat in every word. "I guess I can do that much, at least." Then he looked directly at Leandra. "It'll give me a chance to spend some time with my children."

"Yea! My daddy's the lion," Brittney said, rushing headlong into Nate's arms. "Now you get to rehearse with us every day."

"I sure do," Nate said, his eyes still on Leandra.

She could read that expression well enough to know he was only doing this to show her he could be a good father. Well, she was glad for that, at least.

Chet tugged at her sleeve, bringing her back to reality. "And what about the lamb?"

"What about the lamb?" she asked, wondering what else could go wrong.

"Thelma Nesmith," Chet said, his eyebrows shooting up like bird's wings.

"Yes, Thelma is our lamb. Don't tell me she dropped out of the production, too?"

"Got a cruise for Christmas from her rich son over in Dallas. She'll be leaving in two days. Saw her at the post office today. Said she was gonna call you tomorrow. Might as well tell you tonight, though. We need a new lamb."

Leandra smiled, took a long breath, then nodded. "I'll go through the directory and find someone tomorrow, Chet. No problem."

"You could be the lamb," Brittney said, smiling at Leandra. "My Daddy said you're as pretty as a lamb, 'member?"

Leandra groaned silently while the flush of embarrassment went up her neck and face. "Uh—"

Margaret raised her hand then. "You would make a lovely lamb, Leandra. That has a nice ring—Leandra the lovely lamb. And you have to be nice to the lion."

Making a mental note to seriously strangle her sister-in-law later, Leandra shook her head. "I have enough to do without wearing a lamb's costume."

"But Miss Lea, we need someone tonight to practice," Matt said. "C'mon. You're the same height as Miss Thelma anyway. We won't even have to make another costume."

"I…" Leandra stopped to find too many hopeful gazes all staring directly at her. She'd asked all of them to give of their time and talent, so how could she refuse at this late date? "I guess I could fill in," she said at last, "since we don't have much time and I won't have to learn too many lines."

Chet beamed. "Shucks, all you have to do is sit with the lion and let there be peace on earth, goodwill to men."

"Is that all?" Leandra said, her chuckle just as shaky as her heart felt right now. "A piece of cake."

"This production just got a whole lot more interesting," Margaret said, grinning from ear to ear.

"I'll deal with you later," Leandra told her under her breath as everyone headed to find their costumes for the first dress rehearsal. Then, pulling Margaret to the side, she added, "I thought you wanted me to stay away from Nate Welby and his children."

Margaret glanced around to make sure no one could hear them, then turned back to Leandra, smiling. "That was before I realized you're in love with the man."

"I am not."

"Oh, Leandra, you'd better practice in front of the mirror before you become that little lamb. 'Cause that big, bad lion has a thing for you, and I think you feel the same way about him—and it's not my place to interfere with that, what with peace on earth riding on this entire relationship."

"I'm glad you find this so funny, Margaret."

"It's just good to see you in love at last, even if it is with that cowboy and his brood—better you than me," Margaret told her before she scooted away, her grin still intact.

What does she know? Leandra silently asked herself. Margaret was so shallow and snobbish, she was probably just enjoying Leandra's discomfort. Yet, in her heart, Leandra knew even Margaret wasn't that rotten. Margaret had good qualities, and she had been concerned earlier. It must be the hormones from the new pregnancy making her act and sound crazy.

I am not in love with Nate Welby, Leandra told herself.

Then she looked up and saw Nate standing there, watching her, his eyes that golden, hazel shade of wonder, his hair curling around his face like a lion's mane, his lips twisted in a wry, resigned expression. The man didn't have to roar; she could read him loud and clear.

"I certainly feel like a lamb," she said as she headed to find her own costume. "A lamb about to go to the slaughter."

Mr. Tuttle came up to her then, already dressed as Santa Claus. "The lion and the lamb—Nate and you," he said, his chuckle moving down his big belly. "Now that's worth the price of a ticket."

When Leandra gave him a mock-mean glare, he only winked and smiled, as if he knew exactly what she wanted for Christmas.

Suddenly, this production had taken a new twist.

But Leandra couldn't be sure it would be for the better since she knew in her heart there would be no peace between her and Nate Welby, at Christmas or any time soon.

Chapter Eleven

❧

"And so, right there in front of everyone, Leandra and Nathan both agreed to being the lamb and the lion in the production. It was so funny." Margaret gave a dainty little shrug and giggled behind her hand. "Especially the look on Leandra's face."

Everyone around the dinner table was now looking at Leandra in hopes of a repeat of her shocked expression, no doubt. Well, she wasn't going to give them one. "Margaret, I can't understand why you're so fascinated with all of this. To hear you talk, you'd rather eat nails than be seen in the same room with the Welbys."

Margaret stopped giggling to glance over at Jack for support. "Well, I wouldn't exactly put it that way, Lea. I just had some legitimate concerns about the man and those ragamuffin children, but I have to admit since I've been working with them on this production, I've kinda gotten used to them.''

Colleen smiled, then passed the barbecue sauce to Howard. "Thanks for bringing dinner, Richard. I was afraid with all the last-minute work on the pageant, I'd have to serve grilled cheese sandwiches for dinner."

The pageant rehearsal had been early today, so they were having a casual midweek family dinner consisting of barbecue and all the trimmings from Richard's store. He cooked and smoked his own meat on a huge grill out back. His barbecue, baked beans and potato salad were all famous for miles around. As were his homemade pies.

Taking the hint to change the subject, Richard grinned and saluted his mother. "My pleasure. But I think next week we ought to let Leandra whip up some of her famous dumplings. From what I hear, they keep you full for days to come."

Leandra threw down her napkin. "Okay, that does it. Does anyone else want to tell a cute joke about my personal life? Since it's open season on Leandra, let's hear it. C'mon, don't be shy." She moved her head from side to side, waiting.

The room was suddenly quiet.

Then Mark spoke up. "I'm glad it's you and not me, Sis. When you were away, I was the one who got all the teasing remarks. Seems if you're single and a Flanagan, you don't stand a chance of getting any peace around here."

"Amen to that," Leandra said, Mark's words calming her down a bit. "How did you deal with it, Mark?" she asked him, ignoring Jack's smirk and Richard's grin.

Mark winked, then said, "I just kept right on eating my dinner, and as you know, I always carry some ready reading material. It tends to drown out the superficial small talk."

Michael spoke up then. "We gave up on you long ago, Mark. You're a lost cause. But we're still holding out for little Lea here. *If* she can learn to cook."

"Now, boys," Howard said, his tone soft but firm. "There's no law that says a woman has to know how to cook to get a man. There's more to love than fried chicken and turnip greens."

"Maybe," Richard replied as he stabbed another slice of brisket, "but it sure doesn't hurt."

"What are you worried about, little brother?" Jack asked Richard, laughing. "You can outcook any woman around here—except Mom, of course."

"You saved yourself there, Jack," Colleen replied, one hand on the high chair to hold Philip in and the other on the windup swing right by her chair, where baby Carissa snoozed away to a soft lullaby. Little Corey was in another high chair beside his parents. "And Richard, you're engaged, so you don't count."

Richard chewed his meat, then nodded. "Yeah, and I miss Sheila. I'll be glad when she's done with medical school in Dallas. I'll see her during Christmas, at least.''

Leandra groaned. "So *I'm* the center of speculation these days. How did y'all find out about my dumplings, anyway?''

Everyone spoke at once, each blaming the other.

"Richard told me.''

"Well, Michael told me.''

"Kim called me.''

"Jack told Margaret and—''

"That explains it,'' Mark shouted over the fray. "Margaret can't keep a secret.''

Kim spoke up then. "She kept her pregnancy a secret for four whole weeks.''

Margaret glared around the room, her tiny hands on the table. "I didn't want to spoil *your* being the one with the new baby,'' she said to Kim. "Even though you're ahead of me in the girl department.''

"Sorry.'' Kim stuck out her tongue, then smiled over at her baby daughter. "There's enough joy for both of us, though—boy or girl.''

Margaret nodded to that. "And—I can keep a secret. It wasn't me,'' she told the group. "Richard got the whole thing started about Leandra cooking for the Welbys. It was just so funny, picturing Leandra stringing lights and cooking dumplings. Dumplings, of all things? Lea, why didn't you start with something simple like canned soup?''

Leandra slapped a hand on the table, her patience growing thin. "Okay, okay. I'm trying not to lose my temper, since you are all family and some of you are in a delicate way. But that's enough. Can we change the subject, please?"

Sensing that her daughter was about to cause a scene, Colleen nodded. "Leandra's right. This is none of our business."

"Good," Leandra replied, taking a piece of Texas Toast to sop up barbecue sauce. "I'm glad someone in this room can be tactful."

"Let's change the subject then," Richard replied. "Let's talk about…oh…say…birdhouses. I was expecting to have at least half a dozen to sell before Christmas."

"Birdhouses?" Margaret perked up again. "You mean, like the one on the table in the front hallway. Didn't Nate—"

Leandra stood up then. "Yes, Nate made the birdhouse, for Mama, as a means of repaying *her* for Thanksgiving."

"That was nice," Mark said, a hand on his sister's arm. "Sit down and tell us about it, Lea."

Leandra saw the warning look in Mark's eyes. Ever the calm, detached professor, he was telling her to let it go. If she lost her cool, they would just suspect that she really did have feelings for Nate. But Mark looked as if he already knew that, too.

She sank back down in her chair, defeated. "Yes, Nate makes birdhouses in a little workshop out in his barn. I was impressed with the craftsmanship, so I told Richard about them, hoping that he would display some of them in the store.''

"Which I agreed to do," Richard said, his tone serious at last. "Only I have yet to receive any. Did you talk to Nate about bringing them by?"

"Not really," Leandra admitted. "We didn't get around to discussing it."

"Better things to do," Michael said, giving his wife a knowing look.

Leandra gritted her teeth, then asked God for patience. "I was getting the children to bed and cleaning up the kitchen."

"Dumplings everywhere—" Jack began, but his mother's hand on his arm stopped him. "Oh, back to the birdhouses—do you think Richard could actually sell some of them? I mean, are they that good?"

Richard pointed toward the front hallway. "Have you looked at the one up front? It's truly the work of an artist. I think Nate has real talent."

"So do I," Leandra said, glad to be focusing on something besides her personal feelings for Nate. "I had hoped to convince him to turn it into a business. He could market them and sell them on a regular basis. The money would make a nice nest egg for his children's education."

"He'd need start-up funding, honey," Howard reminded her. "Did you talk to him about that?"

"No," she said. "But I'm glad you're willing to consider lending him the money."

"I told you, we'd already agreed to that years ago," Howard said. "Just too bad he never came back in to secure the loan."

Jack spoke up then. "Lea, I had doubts about Nate, but if Dad thinks it's worth a shot, then I'm behind it. I wish him luck." He smiled over at her then. "And you, too."

"Thank you," Leandra said, feeling better. "Nate would appreciate that. He told me he grew up in an orphanage—he's not used to accepting help from others. He'd want to do this on his own, his way, I'm sure."

Which is why she'd been hesitant about approaching him. He'd probably just turn her down flat. Especially now, when she'd already interfered in his personal life.

Howard gave her a reassuring look. "Nate has a good credit record and he pays his bills. He could get the loan on his own merit, so don't worry about that." Then he pointed a finger around the room. "And of course, this information shouldn't leave this room."

"Of course." Jack nodded, then gave his wife a meaningful look.

"I know the rules," Margaret said, rolling her eyes. "We don't discuss bank customers' finances."

"Even if we are a talkative, informative bunch," Mark teased.

"So when are you going to talk to him, get this

thing rolling?'' Richard looked at Leandra across the table.

"I don't know," she said, aware that everyone was staring at her. "We've both been so busy."

"Well, don't waste too much time," Richard replied. "We've only got a few days before Christmas and this Saturday will be my busiest day. We could use a good, quality product—people love unique handmade things to give for Christmas. Then after the rush, he can see about turning this into a full-fledged business venture."

"I'll try to talk to him soon," Leandra said.

Finally, the conversation drifted to other things. An hour later, dinner was over, leaving Leandra to do the dishes and wonder just when she'd find a chance to talk to Nate. They'd managed to be civil to each other over the last couple of rehearsals, in spite of being thrown together as the lion and the lamb. But it was easy to stand quietly like a demure lamb when you were actually wearing fleece. And she had to admit, Nate made a formidable lion, tall and golden, and almost savage-looking in spite of the cute costume.

The hard part was trying to avoid Nate when they weren't in costume. The man seemed to be everywhere at once. Whereas before, she could usually find him away from the crowd, now he was right in the center of things.

Was it all an act for her benefit, or was Nate beginning to see that he needed to spend more time with his children? Was he actually enjoying himself?

He'd helped with the set, just as he'd promised. He'd nailed his lion's roar on the first try, causing everyone to clap and laugh. He even seemed more comfortable around the members of the troupe, most of whom belonged to Leandra's church. And she'd seen him talking quietly to Reverend Powell on several occasions. He'd even donated his check back to the church, as a means of thanking the Reverend for being so kind to his family.

She'd had to find this out from Margaret of all people!

Because Nate didn't speak to Leandra unless it was absolutely necessary. That made having to stand by him, knowing he was right behind her onstage, even harder to bear. She could sense his presence as surely as she could smell his clean, woodsy soap. She could hear him breathing when the music ended and everything grew quiet.

She could easily reach out and touch him, given how Mr. Crawford had positioned them at the right side of the manger scene, set apart from the donkeys and camels, since they represented peace on earth.

Peace on earth. But no peace in her heart. Not as long as Nate was around.

And not as long as her well-meaning family continued to tease her and question her about her relationship with Nate and his children. She still needed to ask him about those beautiful birdhouses, but Leandra couldn't find the nerve to approach him.

As she climbed in to bed that night, snuggled underneath her mother's old quilt, birdhouses were the last thing on Leandra's mind. That little idea would have to be put on the back burner. Nate wouldn't listen to her idea, not now. Maybe not ever.

And she wouldn't interfere again, no matter how much she longed to be snuggled with him on the couch in front of the fire.

Two days later, Leandra was working at city hall, doing the final paperwork on expenses for the Christmas pageant, when the phone rang.

The receptionist told her, "It's Layla Welby. She sounds really upset."

Wondering what was wrong, Leandra remembered the children had left today's early rehearsal with Mr. Tuttle. Since Nate hadn't been able to get away from work, the kindly old man had promised to see them home safely.

"I'll talk to her," Leandra said, a million worries flowing through her head. While the fourteen-year-old was more than capable of taking care of her younger siblings, Leandra still worried about the children when they were home alone after school, and now all day because of the winter break. Taking a deep breath, she waited for the connection.

After getting the go-ahead from the receptionist, she said, "Layla, it's Leandra. Is everything all right?"

"Miss Lea, you've got to come quick. Daddy's at work, but I called his cell phone and I can't reach him. I left a message with the dispatcher, but Daddy hasn't called back. I didn't know who else to call."

Leandra's heart stopped in her chest, then took up a fast-paced beat. "What is it, honey? Are you hurt? Are Brittney and Matt okay?"

"We're fine, but there's a strange woman knocking at the door. She wants us to let her in but I don't know if I should let her come in the house. She says she's our Aunt Helen."

"Then what's the matter?" Leandra asked, confused. "Surely if she's your aunt—"

Layla gulped, then raised her voice for emphasis. "Miss Lea, you don't get it. We don't have an Aunt Helen."

Chapter Twelve

Leandra tried not to break the speed limit on the way out of town, but the need to get to the Welby place made her push her car to the limit. Trying to think back, she remembered that Nate didn't know his parents or any family, so this woman couldn't be any relation to him.

But what about Alicia's parents? Her mother was dead, but what about her father?

Nate never mentioned his father-in-law. He'd said Alicia's folks were just starting to come around, had just reconciled things with Alicia when she'd been killed. And then her mother had died. Had they tried to made amends with her husband and their grandchildren before that death? Nate hadn't shared much about that with her. And she'd never heard him mention an Aunt Helen.

There was a lot Nate hadn't shared. The man was locked up as tight as a jar of pickled peaches. Sealed. Not to be opened until he was good and ready. And Leandra was beginning to think Nate might not ever be ready to open himself to the world, or God, ever again.

Lord, we need you right now. I need you to help me. I promised I wouldn't interfere again but I have to help Layla. I can't ignore the plea of a child.

She wouldn't ignore Layla's call for help. No matter how mad it might make Nate later. But how could he be mad at her for this? If his children were in danger, he'd want someone to come. Even Leandra.

Bearing that in mind, she pulled the car up to the house, noticing the rented sedan parked in the driveway.

Leandra stopped her own car behind the big sedan. And that's when she noticed the woman pacing back and forth on the front porch.

No wonder Layla refused to let the woman in the house.

Aunt Helen, or whoever she was, was wearing a bright-red Christmas sweater. Rudolph the Red-Nosed Reindeer was plastered across the front in vivid brown and white sequins, and each time the woman moved, Rudolph's shiny red nose blinked brightly. Underneath the thick sweater, she wore black wool pants, impeccably cut, over three-inch-heeled black patent pumps. She had a ring on every finger, in every color of jewel imaginable. Each time she moved her hands, her long red fingernails warred for attention along with her diamonds, emeralds and rubies. Her hair was a silvery-gray and her lips were the same striking red as her sweater. When she heard Leandra's car pull up, she picked up an expensive-looking black patent leather purse that looked more like a suitcase and whirled around, one hand on her tiny hip, to stare down at Leandra.

"And who are you?" the woman asked, looking through her dark sunglasses at Leandra.

Leandra took another calming breath. Up close, the woman was really beautiful. And well preserved. Her makeup was minimal, except for the bright lipstick, and her dark eyebrows arched out over her big eyes in perfect symmetry. She had an air of wealth about her in spite of the fluffy, big hair and the ridiculous sweater. She also held an air of intimidation, as if she were used to giving orders and expecting them to be followed precisely.

"I'm Leandra Flanagan, a friend of the Welbys," Leandra told the woman as she walked slowly up the steps. "And I don't think we've met."

Inside the house, Mutt barked loudly at this intrusion. At least the children had a capable watchdog.

The woman took off her dark shades and shoved them into the bottomless purse, then put out a hand to Leandra. "Well, I'll be. You're a tiny little thing, ain't you? I'm Helen Montgomery."

Leandra took her hand, noted the firm handshake, then gave the woman a slight smile. "Can I help you, Mrs. Montgomery?"

"It's Miss, honey. Never married, never wanted to. But I would like to see my nieces and my nephew in there before I die. If that's all right with *everybody* here." She glared toward the front door, where all three Welby children were peeking out from behind the glass panes, and Mutt's shaggy face could be seen peering over the window seal. "Stubborn lot, ain't they? Got that naturally, I reckon."

Leandra immediately liked Aunt Helen, even if she wasn't quite sure if she could trust her. "I'm sorry. They're just following their father's orders. He's at work and they've been told never to open the door to strangers. That's why they called me."

"But I ain't no stranger," Aunt Helen said, clearly appalled. "I'm a Montgomery, honey." When Leandra could only stand there with a questioning look, the woman added, "Of the *Kentucky* Montgomerys. Land sakes, girl, I'm their grandfather's sister."

Realization dawned on Leandra. "Their grandfather—you mean, Alicia's father?"

"The very one," Helen Montgomery said, bobbing her head. To her hairdresser's credit, not one hair moved when she did it. "Davis Montgomery is my brother."

"I see," Leandra replied, clearly caught between a rock and a hard place. "Well, it's nice to meet you, but I don't know if Nate—"

Aunt Helen threw up her bejeweled hands, causing the gold coin bracelet looped around her tiny wrist to jingle against her aged skin. "Look, Leandra is it? I've been all the way around the world, been traveling for years, moving here and there. Well, I'm tired of traveling. When I got home to Kentucky and asked my brother about these three children—children I've haven't seen in years—I knew I had to come here. My brother is a stubborn old cuss, but I'm even more stubborn than him. And I want to get to know my kinfolk hiding behind that door."

Leandra could feel for the woman. And for the children behind the door, too. Why on earth hadn't Nate and Mr. Montgomery tried to work things out between the two of them, for the sake of those three precious children?

She looked heavenward, thinking, *What should I do, Lord?*

Helen watched Leandra, her intense blue eyes moving over Leandra's face with all the bearing of a hawk. "Look, honey, I don't blame you for worrying. I guess I am a sight, standing here stomping my feet in the cold.'' Then she reached over to take Leandra's hand in hers. ''I'm a churchgoing, God-fearing woman, believe it or not. And I have to do right by those children in there, since my brother hasn't bothered to make amends.'' She held tight to Leandra's hand, then leaned close. ''I don't have any younguns of my own, and my brother is like a brick wall, hard as stone. I'm hoping I can bridge the gap between him and Nate.''

When Leandra saw the genuine concern, coupled with real tears, in the woman's eyes, she knew she couldn't turn her away. ''Nate won't like this,'' she said, thinking he'd blame her for interfering again. But what choice did she have?

''Suga', you let me handle Nathan Welby,'' Helen Montgomery told her, patting her hand. ''Now, can we please go inside out of this cold? I'm gonna take a chill, standing here without my coat on.''

Leandra finally motioned to the children. ''You can open the door, Layla. It's all right.''

The teenager unlocked the big door, then opened it slightly, her gaze traveling over Aunt Helen in a mixture of awe and fear while Mutt tried to claw his way through the crack. ''Are you sure, Miss Lea?''

''Positive,'' Leandra told her, hoping she'd made the right decision. ''Hold Mutt off her, okay?''

Layla opened the door, then told Mutt to get. The

dog sniffed Helen a couple of times, but when she growled at him with arching eyebrows and an amused expression on her porcelain face, he took off running out into the yard.

Leandra guided Helen inside, then turned to the three wide-eyed children standing in a circle in the hallway. "This is Helen Montgomery—your mother's aunt, which makes her your great-aunt."

"So you really are our Aunt Helen?" Brittney asked shyly, her little hands covering her face.

"That I am, suga'," Aunt Helen said as she dropped down on her knees right there on the floor. "Can Aunt Helen have a big ol' hug?"

Brittney glanced up at Leandra for direction. Leandra smiled and nodded. "It's okay, honey."

Brittney rushed into the woman's open arms then, hugging her as if she'd known her all her life. "I never had an aunt before."

"Yes, you did," Aunt Helen replied, looking up at Leandra. "You had me all the time. You just didn't know it. And bless your hearts, you don't remember me, do you?"

The children stood there with blank expressions on their faces.

"My hair's gone more gray since they last saw me," she explained to Leandra with a hand over her mouth.

"No, we don't remember." Layla stood back, still wary, but when Helen rose to give her an unnerving head-to-toe appraisal, she shrugged. "I'm sorry I wouldn't let you in."

"That's all right by me," Helen told her. "You were just doing what your Daddy taught you. And you did a mighty good job of it, too."

Leandra noticed she didn't push for a hug from Layla. Instead, she just reached out and touched a gnarled hand to the girl's cheek. "So like your mother."

Then she turned to Matt. "And you, young man. From what I can tell—and if my memory serves me correctly—you look a whole lot like your papa— handsome fellow."

"How'd you know that?" Matt questioned.

Helen gave him a bittersweet smile. "I was at your mama's—" She stopped, then quickly changed her story. "Your lovely mama, bless her, sent me a picture of the two of them on their wedding day. They sure looked happy." She brightened, then touched a finger to his nose. "And you sure look like Nathan."

"Everybody tells me that," Matt said, his blue eyes big with wonder. "Where'd you get all those rings and bracelets?"

Aunt Helen hooted with laughter, then grabbed Matt to hug him close, the rings and bracelets sparkling and clanking as she did so. "I got them here and there, all over the place. Italy, Morocco, Greece, Japan. I been everywhere and then some. 'Course you'd never know that from this Southern drawl, would you now?'' She stood back then, her gaze moving over the three awestruck children. ''But let me tell you something right now—there is no place like home. And there is nothing like having family.''

''Is that why you came to see us, 'cause we're family?'' Brittney asked, her finger reaching out to touch a dangling bracelet.

''Certainly,'' Aunt Helen replied, taking the colorful beaded bracelet off to drape it around Brittney's tiny arm. ''Hold on to that for me, will you? And don't lose it. It was handmade by my Native American friend in Oklahoma—a full-blooded Caddo.''

''You know Indians?'' Matt asked, fascinated.

''I know *Native Americans,*'' Aunt Helen gently corrected. ''In fact, I'm a walking history lesson. Betcha didn't know you had such a smart ol' aunt, did you?''

''We didn't know we had you at all,'' Brittney said by way of an apology. ''Or we woulda let you in.''

''That's okay,'' Helen said. ''I'm in now, darlin'. And I ain't going anywhere for a good long while.''

Leandra felt tears pricking at her eyes. That might be good news to the children and good for Aunt Helen's sense of family obligation. But she knew one person who might not like having a long-lost relative coming for a holiday visit.

Nate Welby did not like surprises.

And he especially wouldn't like *her* being involved in this one.

Not one little bit.

A little bit further and he'd be home.

Nate pushed the old truck up the highway, looking forward to a hot meal and maybe a warm fire in the fireplace. His pledge to be a better father was actually turning into a real commitment. Maybe prayer really did work.

Except that today, he hadn't been able to take a break from work to attend the rehearsals, and to top things off, the batteries on his cell phone needed recharging. He'd forgotten to charge the thing last night. Too many distractions. Well, he'd make up for those slipups by spending the evening with his children.

He had dinner in the take-out bag next to him in the truck—good food—fresh cooked vegetables and baked chicken from one of his favorite diners out on the highway. He'd make a fire—that had been the ritual since Leandra had started that first one the other night—then he'd read Brittney the Christmas story she'd been begging him to read to her for weeks now. And while the children were out of school for the Christmas holidays, he also planned to help Matt with his math, put in some overtime so his son would be up to speed once school started back up. Adding and subtracting sure had changed since Nate's school days.

But a father could change and adjust with the times, too, he guessed.

It was amazing how he *had managed* to change his schedule, change his whole mind-set, so he could spend more time with his children. It hadn't been as hard as he'd envisioned.

He just had to take it one step at a time, the same way he'd been doing everything since Alicia had died. The dread of coming home each night was slowly being replaced with the need to see his children, to know they were safe and happy, something he'd only monitored from a distance until now.

And he had to admit, it was good to find the house all aglow with holiday lights each night. The bright lights and Christmas decorations chased away the gloom, the bad memories. And maybe this spring, he'd start on that remodeling project he and Alicia had always talked about. He could handle that, if he just took things slow.

Start off slow, work your way up to it.

That's how he viewed everything in life and now his own philosophy was working fine. Except when it came to his feelings about Leandra.

One whole week and he missed her already.

One whole week of being in that huge auditorium with her, with other people all around. And yet, sometimes it felt as if he and Leandra were the only two people in the room. He'd get a whiff of her perfume before she rounded the corner. He'd see her in that funny lamb's costume, white fleece from head to toe, and remember the way she felt in his arms. Then he'd remember the pain in her eyes when he'd accused her of not knowing anything about being a mother.

Lord, I wish I could take that back, he thought now.

But it was too late. Too late for him to admit that Leandra had been a kind, considerate friend to his children, even if she'd never been a mother to anyone before.

"She has the right instincts," he said out loud, the country tune on the radio echoing in his head. "And I shouldn't have been so cruel to her."

If only he could have another chance. He wouldn't rush headlong into it this time around. He wouldn't give her a birdhouse and a kiss. He'd just take things slow, nice and easy, to be sure he knew what he was doing.

Nate turned the truck into the yard, then stopped at the mailbox. Leandra's car was parked at his front door, beside another car he didn't recognize.

Nate shook his head, then slapped a hand on the steering wheel. "I hear you talking, Lord. And I guess You're answering my prayer." A little hesitant, he had to wonder what Leandra was up to now.

And maybe now was his chance to make amends with Leandra, to take things slow and win her over with a steady, sure heart. If only he could be so sure.

One way to find out.

He grinned then. "Please, Lord, all I ask is no more dumplings. A man's stomach can only take so much."

Chapter Thirteen

Standing back to admire the set dinner table, Leandra laughed at how Helen Montgomery had performed her culinary wizardry and kept the children entertained all at the same time. She had produced an exotic pasta dish from a few noodles and some butter, milk and cheese, complete with steamed vegetables and colorful chopped peppers. And she'd let the children help with each step, guiding them, coaxing them, telling them stories every bit as colorful as the food. She also taught them words in several foreign languages as she went along from the main course to some sort of poached dessert involving apples and cinnamon.

For someone who'd never had children of her own, Aunt Helen sure knew a lot about how to control and entertain them.

Much more than I'll ever know.

That thought made Leandra wince, but she tried to keep her own smile intact while she glanced at the clock. Nate was late and she was worried. Dreading the moment he arrived, she was still concerned that he hadn't called to check on the children. Maybe his promise to do better had all been an act, after all.

"And maybe I should have gone home for dinner," she mumbled to herself as she poured milk for the children and iced tea—Aunt Helen's own spiced recipe—for the adults.

She'd planned to do just that—go on home. But Layla had seemed shy and nervous around bubbly Helen. When Leandra had announced she was about to leave, the child had stopped her with an imploring look.

"Can't you stay with us, Miss Lea? You don't have to cook this time."

Aunt Helen immediately picked up on that little tidbit. "Oh, you *are* a close friend, then? Do you cook for Nathan and the children often?"

"I've only know the Welbys a short time," Leandra explained. "They're all involved in the Christmas pageant—"

"And Miss Lea is in charge of everything," Brittney added, grinning. "She says this is going to be the best Christmas pageant the town of Marshall has ever seen."

"Really?" Aunt Helen's perfectly arched brows shot up at that declaration. "I'm thinking I'd better stick around and find out for myself." Her sharp gaze centered on Leandra. "And what about you and Nate?"

Brittney looked up, mouth opened to reply to that particular question, but Leandra shook her head at the little girl and gave her a mock-stern look. Which caused Brittney's bottom lip to jut out in a pout.

"We're friends," Leandra hurriedly explained, then before the children could give their own definitions of what that meant, she shooed them into the kitchen to finish their chores—with Brittney glaring at her the whole time.

But she hadn't fooled Aunt Helen. "Friends, huh? I'm sure Nathan could use a *friend*. The poor man's been out here on his own for too long, from everything I've seen and heard—which hasn't been much since I've been out of the country for months on end. I should have kept in touch more."

Curious, Leandra asked, "What *do* you know about Nathan? Does Mr. Montgomery ever mention Nate and the children at all?"

"Stay for dinner and we'll talk," Helen had replied, her gaze both knowing and understanding.

So now here Leandra stood two hours later, waiting and watching, hoping for answers to all her burning questions, hoping to find some way of understanding Nate and his pain and his anger. She and Helen hadn't had that talk yet. The older woman had somehow managed to keep too busy with cooking and cuddling the children to answer Leandra's earlier question.

Of course, Helen had been more willing to answer all the questions the kids asked—mostly about their beautiful mother. After hearing the tidbits of information and anecdotes Helen dispensed so clearly and lovingly, Leandra felt as if she'd never live up to the image of Alicia Montgomery Welby.

And yet she had so many questions.

Why am I here, Lord? What am I searching for? Why does this family seem to draw me? Why does Nate seem to be the one?

That thought stopped her. The one? *The one for me? The one I could so easily love? Am I crazy?*

"No," Leandra said to herself. "No. I'm just concerned for this family, for these children and their plight." And she did care about Nate. But she wouldn't let her feelings develop into anything other than those of a concerned friend.

She only wanted to help, not hinder.

But would Nate see that, understand when he came home to find a strange woman in his kitchen and Leandra supervising the whole thing?

She heard the front door opening, then whirled to face him. "Nate, hello."

He filled the doorway in his battered leather jacket and worn jeans, a big man with a wavy tawny-colored mane and eyes that seemed to see right through her denials as their depths changed from golden to bronze.

"Hello, yourself," he replied, a bemused smile on his face. Then he sniffed. "That sure smells good, but I brought dinner." He held up the two white take-out bags he balanced in one hand. "If I'd known—"

Leandra didn't miss the implication. She should have called him. "The children couldn't reach you," she tried to explain. "So Layla called me at work."

Nate's expression shifted from a smile to a frown. "The batteries went out on my cell phone and I was away from the site office. I didn't get any messages." Then he continued, "Is everything all right?"

"Yes—no." Seeing the fear and concern in his eyes, Leandra held up a hand. "Everything's fine, Nate. It's just that…the children had a visitor—"

"Who?" At the sound of voices in the kitchen, Nate slammed the door shut with his booted foot, then headed down the hall, past where Leandra stood in the formal dining room. Taking a deep breath, she hurried around the long table to head him off in the kitchen.

But she was too late. By the time she got around the corner, Nate was standing there on the other side of the big kitchen, the take-out bags still in his hand, a look of utter shock and confusion coloring his face. "Helen?"

Helen Montgomery turned around from the stove, the Rudolph nose on her sweater blinking at

Nate just over the ruffles of the white apron she'd donned early. "Hello there, Nathan. How are you?"

Nate stood there, his mouth dropping open as memories assaulted his senses. Alicia had loved her Aunt Helen.

"She's like Mary Poppins," Alicia had told him. "She drops in with all her tales of traveling the world, brings me all sorts of fun gifts and treasures, makes life so much fun, then she leaves again. And I always miss her so much. She'll understand, Nate. She'll understand about us and how much we love each other. She'll come to our wedding. I know she will."

And she had.

Nate closed his eyes to the pain and the memory of Alicia's words. Helen Montgomery had understood almost too well just exactly how much he had loved her niece. Which meant she now knew exactly how much he was hurting. And he didn't want or need the pity he thought he saw in her crystal-blue eyes.

"Well, don't just stand there with your chin on the floor, boy. C'mere and give me a hug."

"She likes to hug," Matt warned his daddy as Nate somehow managed to set the bags on the counter. In two strides, he was across the room, enveloped in Helen's arms.

"Ah, it sure is good to see you again," Helen told him. "It's been too long."

He remembered a big car pulling up to the gravesite. He remembered a petite woman swathed in fur and jewels getting out of the car. She had stood apart from the rest, watching and listening as the minister said one more prayer over Alicia's grave. And she had stayed at the gravesite long after everyone else had left. Nate knew this because he'd found Helen there when he'd gone back later that day. She'd given him a calm pep talk—something about remembering all the good in life—then after a brief, silent hug, she'd climbed in the big car and...left.

And now, here she stood in his kitchen.

"Over three years since the...funeral," Nate said now, conscious of the children watching him. They probably expected him to rant and rave, to throw one of his fits. Truth told, that's exactly what he wanted to do. Then he looked over at Leandra and saw that same expectation in her dark eyes, too.

Well, he'd just have to show them, all of them, that he was trying to change. So he pushed back the dark memories swirling like a wintry fog around his head and mustered up a smile that felt like plastic pulling at his skin.

"What brings you to Marshall, anyway?" he asked Helen as he stood back to look down at her. Even in her high heels, she was still a petite woman.

But what she lacked in size Helen made up for in integrity and determination.

Nate *was* glad to see her.

"I came to see my nieces and that handsome nephew," she said, waving a hand at Matt. Then she looked back up at Nathan. "I had no idea things weren't good between you and Davis...I wish I'd known."

"He doesn't discuss us," Nate said, pulling away.

And *he* never talked about Davis Montgomery. What was the point? They'd both made a feeble attempt, while Mrs. Montgomery was still alive, but once she'd passed on things had changed and Davis had stopped calling. The man had long ago washed his hands of Nate and his own grandchildren.

"Davis is a bitter, self-centered old man," Helen replied, nodding her understanding as she untied her apron.

"Who's Davis?" Matt asked, curiosity widening his blue eyes.

Helen's gaze flew to Nate's face. "You mean to tell me these children don't even *know* about their grandfather?"

Layla glared at Nate then. "We're not allowed to talk about him, or our mother, either."

Nate ran a hand over the five o'clock shadow of his beard, figuring it was payback time and Layla had a lot of resentment stacked against him. "Now, Layla, that's not entirely true—"

"Yes, it is," she replied, capitalizing on having someone's attention at last. "Every time I ask you something about Mama, or our grandfather in Kentucky, you change the subject or tell me you don't want to talk about that right now." Then she lowered her head, breaking Nate's heart with her soft-spoken plea. "We need to know, Daddy. Can we ask Aunt Helen…let her tell us some more stories about Mama and…and our granddaddy?"

"We have a granddaddy?" Brittney asked, her eyes wide, her little hands on her hips. "Nobody *never* tells me anything."

And nobody tried to correct her grammar this time, either.

Nate glanced around to find every eye in the room centered on him. Waves of guilt and remorse washed over him, beating him back even as they cleansed him. How could he have been so blind, so stupid? Why had he denied his children this one thing—the legacy of their mother's memory?

Because he was bitter and unforgiving, pure and simple.

Looking toward Layla for understanding, he nodded. "Honey, you can ask Aunt Helen anything you'd like, okay?"

Surprisingly, the room stayed quiet. Where Nate had expected the three children to bombard their great-aunt with questions, instead they all just stood there, staring at him as if he'd actually changed into the lion they'd forced him to play in the pageant.

Then Layla walked over to him and put her arms around his midsection to give him a hug. "Thank you, Daddy," she said before backing up, her head down. "Supper's ready."

He watched as Helen gave him a quiet, questioning look before she herded the kids through the wide doorway leading to the dining room. Then he turned to Leandra. "I've still got a long way to go, don't I?"

She glanced up at him, pride evident in her eyes. "That was a first step, Nate."

Nate pulled her close then, fighting the need to hug her tight. "I am trying, you know. And I—I need to apologize for the things I said the other night—"

"You don't have to do that," Leandra replied. "I'm just glad you're not angry with me for being here tonight. I didn't want you to think I was interfering again."

He brushed a wayward curl off her cheek. "How could I think that? You came when my children needed you. I'm grateful for that."

She relaxed then, her smile reminding him of how pretty she really was. She was wearing a long, cream-colored sweater over a floral skirt in shades of rich brown and stark gold with a little red mixed in. His autumn woman.

When had he decided she was *his?* he wondered. He couldn't lay claim to her. It wouldn't be fair to either of them. But he sure liked having her in his arms.

Oblivious to Nate's inner turmoil, Leandra laid her head against his chest then looked up with a little chuckle.

"Aunt Helen gave us quite a scare," she said with a shrug and a shake of her head, making her hair fall back across her face. "She is...a very interesting woman."

"She doesn't suffer fools," Nate replied, grinning. "It was just such a surprise."

"I hope you don't mind that I let her in—after giving her the third degree, of course."

"No, I don't mind. It's kinda nice, having her here again." *And having you to come home to,* he thought. Maybe he *could* ease into being with Leandra. He'd been thinking about her all day and now here she was. Just like everything else, if he took things slow...

Leandra laughed then. "And...guess what?"

Nate quirked a brow, enjoying this intimacy, this brief stolen time with her, and wanting badly to kiss that laugh on her beautiful lips. But that wouldn't be taking it slow. That would be another hasty mistake. So instead, he said, "What?"

"I didn't cook dinner."

"Well, amen to that."

When she playfully hit him on the arm, he grabbed her hand. "May I escort you to the table, Miss Flan-again?"

"I'd be delighted, Mr. Welby."

Nate guided her into the dining room, a sense of peace settling over his shoulders. But when he glanced down the table to find Helen's cool blue gaze on him, he instantly regretted that sense of peace.

Alicia's aunt was here for a rare visit, and he'd just been standing in the next room, longing to kiss another woman. What had he been thinking?

And what was Helen Montgomery thinking about him right now?

"I'm thinking our Nate likes you," Helen told Leandra later as they cleared the kitchen. Nate was in the den playing a video game with Matt. Every now and then, they could hear a groan of frustration from the father as his child scored yet another baseball victory.

Leandra glanced over at Helen, trying to decide if the woman was for her or against her. All through dinner, Helen had laughed and chattered away in her rich drawl, mostly talking to the children. But Leandra hadn't missed the keen, interested looks or the knowing expressions Helen had sent toward her and Nate.

Deciding she had nothing to hide or be ashamed of, Leandra nodded, then faced the other woman. "He does like me. We're good friends."

"So, you feel the same about him?"

Leandra focused on the constantly blinking Rudolph nose centered on Helen's left shoulder. "Yes, I do. I like Nate a lot and I adore the children."

Helen stood there, staring, those perfectly sculptured brows lifted in two highly feminine arches. "I see."

"Does that bother you?" Leandra asked, her hands on the counter.

"Should that bother me, honey?" Helen retorted, the keen stare intact.

Leandra knew she was being studied and dissected. "Alicia was a special person," she said, groping for the right words. "Anyone who enters this house can see that. I'm not trying to take her place."

"And anyone who comes here can also see that Nate's let time come to a standstill," Helen replied. "Alicia had such high hopes for this old house. She woulda fixed it up into a showplace."

"But now—"

Helen turned to face Leandra, interrupting her with a hand on her arm. "But now, it's time for Nathan to get on with his life. Is that what you were going to say?"

Leandra faced her squarely, with a clear determination. "No, actually I was going to say that I hope Nate can pour the love he felt for Alicia into raising their children. That should be his top priority. They need their father, to guide them in life and in their faith."

Helen dropped her hand away from Leandra's arm. "And they need their grandfather, too."

Surprised, Leandra lifted her own brows. "Do you think Nate and Mr. Montgomery will ever be able to get past their resentment and anger?"

"Only one way to find out," Helen replied in a low voice. "Get them together."

"Is that why you came here?" Leandra asked, dread in her heart.

"Yes, it is," Helen told her. "And now, I'm even more sure I'm doing the right thing."

"Oh, and why is that?"

"Because of you, young lady. I had my doubts at first, but now I know. I was hoping someone around here would help me bring Nate and my stubborn brother together, and I do believe you're perfect for the job."

Chapter Fourteen

Leandra opened her mouth to speak, then stood there staring across the kitchen counter at Helen Montgomery. "You can't be serious?"

"As serious as cactus thorns," Helen replied, her gaze steady and level. "Now don't tell me you ain't up to the challenge. I thought I had you pegged for a fighter."

Leandra didn't know whether to be flattered or on full alert. "I fight for what I believe in—"

"And don't you believe those children need some attention and love from their grandfather?"

"Of course I'd like to see that happen, but—"

"But what? Afraid Nate will pout and fume? I don't doubt he'll throw a good and mighty fit. But we can't let Davis and him keep us from doing what's right." Helen let out a deep breath. "The good Lord knows those two are as stubborn as the day is long. When I last talked to Davis, he told me he was going to try hard to reconcile things with Nate—''

"How long ago was that?" Leandra interrupted, wondering if Nate had turned the man away.

"About two years," Helen admitted. "I'm as guilty of neglecting them as anyone," she added, shaking her head. "But I had some wanderlust left in my soul. Didn't think I had to worry, since Davis promised me." She stopped, banged a hand against the counter. "I could just shake both of 'em."

Leandra understood completely, but she had to make Helen see that she wasn't the one to help bridge this gap. "I don't think Nate would appreciate me being involved in this. He's already made it clear that I should let him raise his children the way he sees fit."

"He can't see past his grief and his love for Alicia, honey," Helen returned. Then the fire in her crystal-blue eyes softened at the expression of pain and discomfort Leandra couldn't hide. "'Course, you know all about that, don't you?"

"Yes, I do," Leandra said. "I care about Nate, but I've accepted that we can't be anything more than just friends. And I have to tell you, I'll be leaving Marshall right after Christmas."

Helen's pout was pure disapproval. "And why's that?"

"I have to go back to Houston. I've got to find

another job or I'll have to give up my apartment, my life back there.''

"Are you so sure you want to go back?" Helen asked, her brows arching in that disconcerting way again. "Honey, we just met and I don't know all the details, but the way you look at Nathan Welby—well, I get the impression you'd like things around here to change in a positive way, with you being part of the positive. Am I wrong?"

Leandra couldn't answer that. If she spoke the words out loud, she'd melt into a helpless puddle of defeat. Instead, she said, "As I told you, Nate and I have agreed to be friends. And...I have to make some decisions regarding my future. I've held off long enough."

Helen lifted her chin, then gave Leandra a side-ways glance. "Sometimes, we just have to trust in the Lord and let things take place in a natural kind of way."

"You sound like my mother."

"We're older, wiser, and we've got the blessed assurance of God's wisdom," Helen replied. "Now, can I count on you?"

"Count on her for what?" Nate asked from the hallway. He strolled into the kitchen, a slight smile on his face. "The munchkins and the Mutt are all in bed at last, but what are you two up to?"

Helen gave Leandra a warning look. "I want to get to know Leandra a little better and I'm counting on her to come around more while I'm visiting," Helen said. "To help me adjust."

"Just how long are you planning on staying?" Nate asked, a teasing light in his eyes.

"Oh, you know what they say," Helen countered. "After three days..."

Nate grinned, then put an arm around her shoulders. "You can stay as long as you want, you know that."

"Mighty generous of you," Helen said, hugging him close. "How about through next week—at least till Christmas?"

Nate glanced over at Leandra. "That'll be just fine. We could use some cheerful company around here for the holidays."

"Then it's settled," Helen said, lifting her arm away. "And on that note, I'm going to bed. Layla said I could bunk with her."

"She's up there getting your spot ready right now," Nate told her. "Sleep tight."

"Don't let the bedbugs bite," Helen finished. Then to Leandra, "It was good to meet you, suga'. Hope to see you soon." She leaned close. "And don't worry about that other. I'll take care of it."

"What other?" Nate asked, a mock frown on his face.

Helen handled him with a wave of the hand. "Just Christmas surprises—nothing for you to be concerned about just yet."

"Thanks," Leandra told the other woman, relief

flooding her senses. "I'm sure we'll see each other again."

After Helen went upstairs, Nate turned to Leandra. "Wanna walk out to the barn with me? I need to check on Honeyboy, make sure he's all warm and toasty in his stall."

Surprised at the invitation, Leandra told her heart to slow down. It took off so fast, she was sure it skipped a few beats. "Sure," she said, a little breathless. "Let me get my coat."

The night was clear and cold, with a full glowing moon and a million silver-blue stars hanging against a velvet-soft sky.

Nate took her hand to help her down the steps. "Watch that rotten board," he said, grinning up at her.

"I remember it well," she replied, her hand in his. His fingers felt so strong, so sure wrapped around hers.

Together, they slowly made their way down the sloping yard toward the big barn.

"I'm glad you stayed for supper," Nate said. "I didn't like how we left things the other night."

"I shouldn't have been so pushy," she replied. Hoping to make him understand, she added, "You're a very good father—I didn't mean to imply otherwise."

They reached the barn door and Nate turned to face her. "But you were right about a lot of things. I just didn't want to hear the truth."

Longing to ask him what really *was* the truth, Leandra kept her mouth shut. It was enough that they'd formed a tentative bond for now. She didn't want to ruin another evening with Nate. And she reminded herself, now might be the perfect time to bring up the possibility of showcasing some of his birdhouses at Richard's general store. That was a safe, businesslike topic, at least.

She waited as Nate turned on the dim overhead light then tugged her toward Honeyboy's stall in the back.

The big horse snorted hello then pushed his nose over the stall to get a closer look at them.

"He's a beautiful animal, Nate," Leandra said, coming close to let the horse nuzzle her hand. "I think he wants a late-night snack."

Nate obliged by giving Honeyboy a handful of grain. "Not too much now, fellow."

After making sure the horse was comfortable and warm, Nate started back toward the front of the barn.

But Leandra held back. "Nate, could I see some of your work? Maybe some of the birdhouses?"

Giving her a sly grin, he teased. "Want to see my etchings, huh?"

Leandra's blush of warmth sent the chill in the old barn right out the door with her good sense. Ignoring the tingling sensations racing down her spine, she tried to remain serious. "I want to see what you do out here every night. What you've created."

He glanced around, hesitant. "Oh, I don't know about that. There isn't much to see, really."

Leandra pushed ever so gently, determined to show him that his talent shouldn't be hidden away. "C'mon, if all of your designs look like the one you gave my mother, then I'd say there's a lot to see."

"It's just a hobby," he told her. But he took her by the hand even as he said the words. "I don't expect to make anything out of it."

Sensing an opportunity, Leandra said, "Richard was really impressed with our birdhouse. He said he could probably sell dozens of them in his store—what with the Christmas rush and everything."

"Is that a fact?" He grinned, then took her over to the workshop area. He stood silent for a minute, as if remembering, then said, "I don't know if that's possible."

"But wouldn't you like to see?"

Nate turned to face her again. "What's cooking in that pretty head of yours, Leandra?"

She smiled, her eyes widening, her tone hopeful. "I really think you have talent and I also think you should try to promote that talent. I should know. This is what I did for a living back in Houston."

Nate put his hands in the pockets of his leather jacket. "Now *there's* something *I'm* curious about.

Tell me about Houston. What happened back there?''

So Nate had found an opportunity to seize the moment, too, Leandra mused. Well, maybe it *was* time she told him the truth. Maybe if he could see that she trusted him enough to let him in on her own failings, he'd learn to trust her in return.

"It's not a pretty story," she said in a low voice.

He reached out to touch her cheek, the warmth of his fingers gliding over her skin making her feel all flush inside. "I want to know."

Deciding to push one more time, she said, "If I tell you all about it, will you show me the rest of your birdhouses?"

"You drive a hard bargain," he replied. Then he nodded and lifted her chin with the pad of his thumb. "Start talking."

Leandra swallowed, suddenly aware that the old barn had become silent and still, waiting. An occasional creak and Honeyboy's contented snort now and then finally broke the silence, but Nate's warm gaze on her kept Leandra from hearing anything over the beating of her pulse.

"I worked for a large advertising firm," she began, her hands in the pockets of her black wool topper. "I did a good job and soon I was promoted to senior account executive."

"What does a senior account executive do exactly?" he asked in that teasing drawl.

She smiled, tried to relax. "I solicited major

companies to advertise through us. We designed their ad campaigns and took care of all their public relations and marketing, working with their in-house departments, of course.''

He stepped closer. "Of course."

Trying hard not to be distracted by his ever-changing eyes or his intense expression, Leandra continued. "As I said, I was very good at my job and soon, I was making more money than I ever dreamed possible."

"And you became that city woman you always wanted to be."

She didn't miss his frown.

"Yes, that was me." She shook her head, turned to lean against a large support post. "And I made so many mistakes." She let out a sigh, wishing she could just go back and change things. But it was too late for that. And she needed to get this out in the open. "My boss—the president and owner of the company—was an older man named William Myers—" She stopped, remembering that just a few days ago, she'd let it slip to Nate that she'd been involved with her boss. Now she was morti-fied that he wanted to hear the whole story.

"Go on," Nate said, his gaze level, his expres-sion neither condemning nor questioning.

"We worked together on one of the major cam-paigns and after that...we started dating." She shrugged, tossed her hair off her face. "At first, it was just platonic—someone to be seen around town with—companionship. He'd never been married and he was content to remain a bachelor. I was convenient, since I didn't make demands on him. And I wasn't ready for marriage or children either, so our relationship worked for both of us.''

"What a perfect setup."

She gave him a wry smile. "Or so it seemed.'' Pushing hair off her face, she began again. "We went along like that for a while. Then something changed in William. He started wanting more and I thought I might be ready to give it, but I wasn't sure if I loved him enough to make such a commitment. I thought he wanted to get married.''

Shaking her head, she added, "I got this silly notion that I'd be the wife of a successful executive. I'd live in the big mansion on the hill, have fancy cars, eat at the finest restaurants—all the things I'd dreamed about growing up. But suddenly, having a family *did* seem important. And yet, part of me kept saying, 'But you don't want to get married. You don't want children. You want to enjoy life, stay single.'''

He stopped her there. "Why was that so important, staying single, not having children?''

Letting out a sigh, she replied, "Because I grew up in this large, loud family. I watched my mother always cooking and cleaning, and doing the car pool thing, the volunteer work with the PTA and the church. I guess I just needed some space, away from all the commotion, away from my overbearing, lovable brothers.'' Shaking her head, she laughed. ''I don't know how my mother does it. I only knew I didn't want to find out.''

She paused, took another breath. ''So what you said the other night—''

''I was wrong to assume that about you,'' Nate interrupted, anger clouding his face in the moonlight from the partially open door. ''You'd make a great mother.''

Leandra almost bolted then. The soft, husky catch in his voice only made her want to give in and fall into his arms. She wanted *him* to give her that chance to prove she could be a good mother.

Holding on to the pole behind her, she pushed back the need to be consoled and reassured. ''It doesn't matter. You were right. At one time, I only wanted wealth and success. I thought those things would fulfill me, make me complete, give me the world I'd always thought I was missing living here in this small town.'' She let go of the pole, dropping her hands at her sides. ''But I was so wrong. And soon, all my big, shallow dreams were thrown right back in my face.''

''What happened?'' Nate asked, frustration playing across his face. ''I can't stand this—just spit it out.''

She had to smile at his impatience, but she dreaded telling him the truth. Finally, after a long deafening silence and the intensity of his unwavering gaze, she blurted the truth. ''William didn't ask me to marry him, Nate. He asked me to move in with him, to live with him.''

She watched Nate's face for his reaction. Would he turn away from her, disgusted with her superficial whinings?

"Let me get this straight," he said, his voice quiet. "The man didn't want to marry you, yet he wanted to...to..."

"As my mother would say, he wanted me to live in sin with him."

"And you turned him down flat."

Yet again, he'd somehow managed to make her smile in spite of her misgivings. It had been a statement, not a question. Nate somehow knew exactly what she'd done, which meant he thought she had *some* good qualities, at least.

"Yes, I did. Because I realized that contrary to all my sophisticated pretentious thinking, I was really a country girl at heart. And a Christian. I couldn't do something that went against my moral fiber."

"So you quit."

Another statement. Another sweet assumption.

"No." She actually managed a chuckle. "I broke things off and concentrated on my work. But William couldn't take rejection, especially from someone he considered an underling. So...he started harassing me at work, making demands on me, criticizing everything I did. I was still the same— still hardworking, dedicated. I handled several exclusive accounts but one by one, they were snatched from me and handed over to someone else.''

Nate groaned. ''What did you see in this weasel, anyway?''

''I started asking myself that same question,'' she replied. ''I had been so blinded by ambition, by success, that I'd almost thrown away everything I believed in, just to say I'd made it in the world. I actually might have married William without loving him, if only he'd asked me.''

''You can do much better than that kind of creep,'' he said, anger justifying his words.

Nate's self-righteous defense of her only endeared him to Leandra even more. ''Yes, I know that now,'' she admitted. ''And each time he punished me, I saw more and more that I didn't really belong in that kind of world. A world where money and power are put ahead of people and integrity. The final straw came when he gave me my annual evaluation. I didn't get a promised raise, and two of my best accounts were handed to another woman in the office—a woman he'd just started dating a few weeks before that.''

''Scum,'' Nate mumbled under his breath.

''Exactly,'' Leandra replied. ''I saw the pattern, realized I'd been a complete idiot, and understood that he'd only wanted me as a decoration. He never really cared about me.'' She dropped her head then. ''I felt so used, so dirty.

''But the worst of it was—I'd been using him

too, for my own purposes. When I stopped to analyze my own motives, I felt empty, sick at heart. I'd been so selfish, trying to control my life, fighting against the very instincts that make me who I am inside. I'd turned away from God, turned away from the love and support of my family, neglected my own soul's nurturing, and I came very close to making a big mistake. William and I had treated what should have been a deep and abiding love and respect between a man and a woman with little more than a casual passing. When I thought of the love my parents feel for each other, even after all these years, well...I knew I'd been so wrong.

"I went home one night, stood in the middle of my upscale, ritzy apartment, and saw the emptiness all around me. I realized I was just as bad as William. So I did some heavy praying and after pacing the floor all night, I reached a decision."

Drained and exhausted, tears misting her eyes, she looked up at Nate. "The next morning, I turned in my resignation and...I came home."

Nate pulled her into his arms, hugging her with such a fierce warmth and strength, Leandra knew at that moment that she had indeed come home. At last.

Nate stroked her hair gently. "No matter what you think you did, the man had no reason to ruin your career or treat you that way. You should sue him."

"Sure I could sue him for harassment, and bring

out the fact that I had been dating him.'' Leandra stood back and shook her head. ''He'd make mince-meat of me, convince people that I'm just a woman scorned. I won't put my family through that kind of pain. I just want to forget the whole thing, get on with my life.''

Nate stepped close again, his hands still caught in her hair. ''So what are you going to do now?''

Leandra's heart knew the answer, but she couldn't voice what her heart was shouting at her. ''I don't know. I only know that…I've changed in the last few months. I *do* want the simple, basic things—a home to come to whether I'm hurting or happy, and a family that loves me, no matter what, and no matter the size of that family.''

''Anything else?'' he asked, so close now she could see the tiny flecks of brown and green in his cat eyes. And a gentle yearning.

Did she dare tell him her sweet dream? Her fragile hope?

''I'd like to have a family of my own someday,'' she said, thinking that would cover everything without revealing anything.

But Nate had a determined, awe-filled look on his face, a look that matched her own hope even while it scared her. ''What made you change your mind, city woman?''

Hesitant, she said, ''I told you—I realized that William and I had been—''

''All wrong,'' he interrupted, his face lined and

shadowed from the muted overhead light, his big hands pushing through her hair so she couldn't look away. "I understand that, but I think there's more. So I'll ask you again. What made you change your mind, Lea?"

He'd called her Lea. The intimacy of that, the gentle way he'd said it, brought her a kind of joy she'd never experienced before with any man.

"I think you know the answer to that," she whispered as she reached her arms around his shoulders.

He tugged at her hair, urging her to him. "I want to hear you say it."

Leandra looked up at him, a thousand wishes merging into a silkened thread of need in her heart. "You," she said at last, breathless. "*You* changed my mind, Nate."

His expression shifted from determined to doubtful, and yet he held her there. For a long time, Nate just stared down at her, his gaze traveling like a whisper over her face, finally touching on her lips.

And Leandra held her breath, waiting for the war inside him to end. Waiting for him to find some sort of peace.

"*I'm* no good for you," he said even as he pulled her close. "Maybe you *do* belong in that big mansion on the hill."

Leandra could almost read his mind. He was afraid, because Alicia had given up everything to be with him, and to his way of thinking, she'd paid dearly for that choice. Could he risk that again with Leandra? Could he ask her to do the very same?

Yes, she would risk a lot by falling in love with Nathan Welby. This wasn't safe or shallow. This was very real, more deep and abiding than any form of friendship. And Nate knew that better than anyone. Was he testing her? Giving her one last chance to walk away?

She didn't want to walk away. She wanted... *Oh, Lord,* she prayed, *give me the strength to be worthy of this man. And please, give him some peace, some comfort.*

"I belong right here," she told him, a hand touching his cheek. "If only you'd let me in."

Nate closed his eyes, kissed her hand, then moved close to kiss her lips, testing her, demanding proof and draining her of all willpower. Leandra pushed a hand through his thick, wavy hair, savoring the coarse feel of it, savoring the sweet taste of his lips. This couldn't be wrong, not when it felt ten times more right than anything she'd had with William.

And yet, she could still sense the hesitancy in Nate. As much as he needed her, he didn't want to let go completely.

Leandra pulled away to give him a beseeching look. "What can I do to convince you?"

He looked down at her, the tenderness and doubt in his eyes only adding to her own fears and needs. She wanted so much to wipe away all his pain.

"Just keep kissing me," he finally said, his mouth capturing hers again.

The kiss was long and sweet, filled with a thousand sensations and a thousand hopes. Leandra could feel the shift in Nate as he slowly gave in to what they both felt so strongly. With a deep longing, she returned his kiss, hoping this tender thread that had somehow bonded them wouldn't be broken again.

When he finally lifted his head, Nate took a breath and grinned, sighing as he managed to regain control. "I think I'd better show you those birdhouses."

Leandra's heart glowed with a warm fire and a burst of white-hot joy. Nate trusted her, at last.

Chapter Fifteen

"This is amazing," Leandra told him much later as she stood admiring the rows and rows of birdhouses Nate had made. He'd hidden them away on a high shelf underneath a canvas tarp. But they needed to be out in the world. Quickly, she counted at least twenty tiny houses of various shapes and sizes, some made out of pine, some made out of oak. A cypress one here, complete with Spanish moss, a pirogue—a boat draped in fishing net—and a tiny Cajun sign that read *laissez les bons temps rouler*—let the good times roll—hanging over the door. A cedar one over there, rustic and fresh smelling, the tiny trees surrounding it a miniature of the tree from which he'd built the house. Each house had its own distinctive character. Each looked like a home. The careful details, the ornamentation, all spoke of a gifted hand.

She whirled around, dancing toward him. "Nate, we have to show these to someone. You—you have such talent."

He shook his head. "I told you, it's just a hobby. Something to pass the time away."

Something to keep the memories away, too, Leandra thought. This man, this gentle, sweet, sad man, built miniature houses for God's small creatures, to replace the real home he thought he'd lost when his wife died.

And yet, his own house sat crumbling around him.

She had to make him see the connection, the correlation between the two. She had to make him let this go, give this gift to others, so that he could find the gift of forgiveness and grace that God readily offered to him.

"Nate, please," she began, asking God to help her do this the right way, "let me display some of these in Richard's store, just to see."

He shook his head again. "I don't think I'm ready for that."

She watched his face, saw the pain centered there in the lines of fatigue around his eyes. His smile didn't reach into those golden eyes. And he refused to look at her.

"And why not?" she finally asked, needing to hear what was in his heart. "Why would you want to keep making these wonderful houses and not show them off to the world?"

He stalked around the workbench, a dark frown marring his face. "I don't think people would be interested. They're just birdhouses, Leandra."

"They're art," she replied, determined to make him open up, one way or another. It would be the only way he'd ever come to her, and back home to God, completely.

"I don't know about art," he said, lowering his head to gaze at her, a stubborn, proud expression giving him the lionlike quality she'd seen in him when they'd first met. "I just know I like to stay busy, work with my hands. It's doodling, playacting, something to do."

"Playacting," she repeated. "Building little homes, beautiful little objects with such exquisite detailing. Why wouldn't you want to share that gift with others?" Then she tossed him the one question he wasn't ready to answer. "You gave *my* family one. Why did you do that, if you don't want anyone to see them?"

Nate stared at the woman across from him, his heart near bursting with the need to pull her back into his arms. But his whole body was stiff with resistance. So he told her a lie. "I was just returning a kindness, nothing more."

Why *had* he given Leandra and her mother the birdhouse? He'd wanted her to have something beautiful from him, something that was a part of his heart, his past, his dreams. He hadn't been able to give that gift to anyone, until now. And he still wasn't sure why he'd done it for Leandra, except that it had seemed important at the time.

Oh, Lord, what's happening to me? Is this Your answer, Your way of telling me to snap out of it?

Well, he didn't want to snap out of it. He'd taken this too far, way too far with his gifts and his kisses. But earlier, Leandra had felt so good, so right, in his arms. Earlier, he'd told himself it was okay to hold her, to kiss her, to listen to her innermost secrets. He'd asked her to tell him everything. He'd needed to know.

He'd given in to this—this opening up of his own wounds, his own festering regrets and secret yearnings. He had no one to blame but himself.

And yet, he wanted to lay blame at God's door, just as he'd done for so long. That was so easy, so simple. It took all the responsibility away from Nate's own shoulders.

And he wanted to be angry again, to hide the hurting need inside his heart. To hide the truth.

"What are you trying to say, Leandra?" he asked now, a cold shield of frustration making the question edgy and sharp. *Please, God, give me something to be angry about.*

She looked as frustrated as Nate felt. "I'm trying to make you see that you have a gift, a talent. Why are you letting it go to waste? Why are you hiding it away underneath a dirty canvas? Why don't you open it up and let it out in the world? Is it because Alicia's not here to share it with you?"

His head came up then, but he couldn't begin to speak. But Leandra had a lot more to say.

She stopped long enough to take a breath, then said, "I know about the loan, Nate. You and Alicia came to my father—I know this was your dream. It can still happen. My father will help you in any way he can—"

"No."

Okay, he had something to be angry about now. It should feel good, but instead he felt miserable, alone, suffering. At least *that* was familiar.

"How dare you?" he said, halting her with a shaking hand up in the air between them.

With each question she'd hurled across the workbench at him, Nate's anger had grown until all he could see was the red pain of grief—his old friend—there in the muted light of the barn. But now, oh now, blessed, welcome rage replaced the grief. This time, she'd gone too far.

"What do you mean?" Leandra asked, going quiet. "I was just trying to explain, to help—"

"I don't want your help," he told her, shouting so loudly the rafters shook and Honeyboy let out a whinny of protest. Pointing toward the birdhouses, he said, "That was *our* dream—Alicia's and mine. How dare you—you discussed it with your father? He had no right to tell you anything about what Alicia and I wanted, no right."

"He only told me when I insisted—about the

birdhouses,'' she tried to explain. "He...we want to help you, Nate.''

The anger flared like a torch in the night, burning at the emotions he'd tried to deny. "I don't need your help. Can't you understand that? Can't you see that I loved my wife and no woman can ever replace her?''

No matter how that woman makes me feel!

And then he knew, he'd succeeded once and for all. He'd hurt Leandra beyond repair. Yet, he felt no victory. The anger, the grief, felt as dry and bitter as dust and dead leaves in his mouth. It cut to his very core as he watched her face, saw the pain there, saw the hurt, the shock, the realization.

"Yes, I can see that,'' she said, her voice so quiet, so raw he had to strain to hear her. "I see everything, Nate. It's all very clear to me.'' She waved her hands toward the tarp, then turned and yanked it down, away from the clutter of the birdhouses. "I can see that you want to hide away here in this old barn, away from your pain, your regrets, away from the knowing faces of your own children. And I feel so sorry for you, so sorry.''

"I don't need your pity—''

Leandra pivoted, her eyes all fire and flash now. "Oh, it's not pity. It's...a sad kind of acceptance. You don't want to be happy, really happy, ever again. You want to stay hidden away, covered up, like your precious designs, because if you come out into the light, if you ask me, or my family, or God

Himself, for help, then you'll be betraying Alicia. But worse, you'll be tearing down that big wall of grief you're hiding behind."

She came around the table then, her hands at her side, her expression calm and rigid. "If you let go of that grief, you'll have to come clean. You'll have to let go of Alicia's memory and actually forgive yourself. But you can't do that. You can't accept that you're really worthy of forgiveness."

The silence encrusted them in a cold, brisk snap, like a branch caught in a frozen wind.

Then finally Leandra spoke again. "But you're so wrong, Nate. Your children think you're worth forgiving. They just don't know if you can ever forgive *them* for being a part of their mother. Do you know that Layla thinks you hate her? Do you?"

His heart caught in his chest, weighing him down so he had to catch his breath. "Stop it—"

"No," she shouted. "I won't stop it. I won't let you continue to punish yourself this way. Forget the artwork, this goes deeper. You need help, Nate. But then, I've tried to help you, haven't I?"

When he didn't answer, she said, "Well, it's your turn. Now it's all up to you. *You* have to find the strength to help yourself. And…*you* have to ask God, really ask Him from your heart, to give you grace. You have to learn to love yourself again, before you can love your children…or…me."

"I don't love you," he shouted, wagging a finger

at her, denial his last true weapon. "I don't...love you."

"I know that," Leandra said, simply, quietly. Then she turned away and headed for the door.

Nate watched her go, his heart calling for her to come back, come back.

A still, silent emptiness penetrated the old barn. The building was full of clutter, full of colorful, decorative little houses.

Empty houses.

Just like his soul.

Was this how Leandra had felt that night, standing all alone in her apartment? He remembered what she had told him, and then he remembered how she'd handled her failings. She'd come home to her family and her Heavenly Father, seeking solace, seeking grace.

But Leandra had much more courage than he could ever possess. He stood there, paralyzed, afraid of his own emotions, and wondered what to do next. He wanted Leandra, but he couldn't have her.

"I don't deserve to be happy again," he said into the stillness.

Then a piercing shard of moonlight from the partially opened door shot through the night, coloring Nate's creations in a glow of pure translucent beauty. He looked up, his gaze never wavering from that one bright spot. Standing there, he remembered Leandra's words earlier about coming out into the light. But he was so afraid, so afraid.

Then suddenly, he understood. He'd been praying, but not with his whole heart. He hadn't let go; he'd wanted to control the blessings God gave out to him. Nate had been in charge, so sure he didn't need anyone, so sure he could never love another woman again. So sure he didn't need God's help or guidance in raising his children. And he'd failed miserably.

"God, dear Lord, help me, help me," he said at last. Then he fell to his knees and cried the tears of the weary.

"I do love you," he finally said, the confession cutting through his throat like bramble as he fought against both it and his tears. "I do love you." He was not only talking to God, but he was telling Leandra the truth at last.

Realization and acceptance poured over Nate like baptism water, drenching him, cleansing him, purging him of all the hostility, all the blame and guilt, all the self-hatred and self-denial.

He wiped his face and got up, then rushed to the door. "Leandra, come back—I do love you."

But she was already gone.

Christmas Eve. Leandra glanced out the kitchen window, wondering if the predictions of snow the weatherman had hinted at would come true. It rarely snowed in East Texas, but the weather had been bitterly cold and icy all week and a huge winter storm was bearing down on them from the northwest. Would they have a white Christmas?

"Honey, do you want some hot chocolate?" Colleen asked as she walked into the kitchen. "Before you head out for the pageant?"

Leandra turned to face her mother, hoping the drained, tired expression she'd seen in the mirror just minutes before was well hidden behind the smile she tried to muster. "Sure, Mom. That sounds great."

"The last performance," Colleen said as she automatically measured milk, cocoa, cinnamon, sugar and vanilla into a big pot on the stove. "Sit down while I stir. I'll be done soon."

Like a sleepwalker, Leandra obeyed her mother. One more night, and then it would all be over. The strain of the last few days was catching up with her. Only through sheer determination and constant prayer had she made it through the first couple of performances.

But her heart wasn't in the program. She kept remembering how angry Nate had been, how he'd declared he only loved Alicia. Leandra had rushed out of that old barn, determined to never set foot on the Welby property again. But when she'd reached her car, she'd fallen against the cold steel and metal, her head in her hands, and cried tears of frustration and anger.

The night had been so cold. And she'd felt so

alone. She'd actually thought she'd heard Nate calling to her just as she opened the car door. But it had only been the wind, moaning a forlorn, lonely whine.

Now, she was sleepwalking. Was this how Nate felt each day as he pined away for Alicia? Only half alive, only going through the duties and motions of each day, his soul lost in the past, lost in what might have been?

The production had been a success, with each actor playing his part, each song right on key, each drama clear and deeply moving. Everyone had complimented Leandra on doing a good job.

But she had to wonder, could they all see the pain, the heartbreak in her eyes, in her gestures, in her movements? Did they know that each night as she stood there beside Nate, both of them in their costumes, that he had broken her heart beyond repair? Had anyone noticed how she avoided Nate's gaze, how she managed to ignore him when he called her name, how she managed to stay on the other side of the stage until it was time for them to play their parts?

Did anyone notice that she was so in love with him she could barely breathe?

Someone had noticed.

"Lea, we need to talk," Colleen said in a quiet firm tone. "Here's your cocoa."

Leandra glanced up, completely unaware that her

mother had even finished making the hot drink. "What is it, Mom?"

"Sweetie, I'm worried about you. You haven't been yourself over the last few days. Are you worried about going back to Houston?"

Leandra shook her head, the effort of moving almost too much to bear. "No. I'm ready to go back. I need to get back to my life." *Except that I don't have a life anymore.*

Colleen settled on a stool across from her daughter. "I had so hoped you'd decide to stay here. Chet could use your help down at city hall—said he'd ask the city council to give you a raise and make you marketing and public relations director for the city. Have you thought about that?"

Leandra nodded, tried to muster up a smile. "Chet's mentioned it a few times. He wants an answer, but I don't think—"

"It's Nate, isn't it?" Colleen asked, her hand falling across Leandra's. "Honey, tell me what happened."

Leandra knew she could pour her heart out to her mother, just as she'd done when she'd first come home from Houston, and Colleen would listen and try to advise her, without condemnation, without judgment, but always with a mother's strong, fierce love. But where to begin?

"Mom, how do you know when it's real?"

Colleen looked confused for a minute, then said, "You mean love?"

Leandra nodded, unable to say more.

Colleen smiled, patted her hand, then let out a long sigh. "Love is hard to explain, honey. It's a kind of magic, but not like that in a fairy tale or like a magician pulling flowers out of a hat. Love, true love, involves the magic of faith, in knowing that this was part of God's plan. It comes from the heart, and it's more powerful than anything on earth."

Leandra looked up then, tears streaming down her face. "More powerful than a man's love for his dead wife?"

"Oh, honey." Colleen came around the counter to take Leandra in her arms. "I thought as much. You're in love with Nate, aren't you?"

Leandra nodded against the sweet warmth of her mother's old wool cardigan. "But he says he doesn't love me."

"Do you believe him?"

Leandra pulled away, wiped her eyes. "No. I think he does love me, but he's too afraid to admit it. He thinks he'll mess things up, the way he believes he did with Alicia. He feels so much guilt."

Colleen pushed a strand of damp hair off Leandra's face. "You know, honey, it's Christmas. A time of miracles and love. Give Nate some time to settle things with God. If he cares about you, he won't let you go back to Houston." She stood back then, her smile reassuring. "And something tells me he does love you, very much. I had that figured the day you brought that beautiful little birdhouse home.''

''I wish I felt as sure as you do,'' Leandra said. Because time was running out.

Chapter Sixteen

He didn't have much time left. Nate pushed the old pickup up the highway, headed for town. It was Christmas Eve and he wanted to spend it with his children and the woman he loved.

Leandra.

Would she ever be able to forgive him?

He'd sent Layla and the young ones on with Mr. Tuttle and Aunt Helen—those two had sure become fast friends—so they could get ready for the last performance of the pageant. But not before Helen had come out to the barn to give him a good talking-to.

"How come you stay cooped up out here so much?"

Not wanting to go into detail, Nate grunted. "I work out here."

"Yeah, so I hear. Every night, it seems." When

he didn't respond, she asked, "So what are you doing out here on Christmas Eve?"

"I'm working on something—a Christmas gift for a friend."

"And would that friend happen to be named Leandra Flanagan?"

Nate had given up trying to hide his feelings. If he'd learned one thing since falling for Leandra, it was that the truth would come out, one way or another. "Yes, it's for Leandra. And Helen, I'm sorry if you don't approve, but—"

"But what? Who said I didn't approve? I like that girl. She's pretty, honest, and...she loves your children. What more could I ask?"

Surprised, Nate smiled for the first time since he and Leandra had parted. "You never cease to amaze me, Helen."

"Are you in love again, Nathan?"

"Yes," he told Helen. Then he showed her what he was making.

Helen nodded her approval, a smile gentling the frown that had her eyebrows standing straight up on her face. "Well, she hasn't been around since the other night, and she sure keeps her distance at the Christmas pageant. You two been fighting?"

"Something like that."

"You're a stubborn one, Nate Welby."

"Too stubborn for my own good." He looked up then, the honesty making him feel edgy, almost dizzy. "I don't want to lose her."

Helen punched the sleeve of his denim jacket. "Well, when are you gonna give this to her, and for land sakes, when are you gonna tell her you love her?"

"Tonight," he replied. "Tonight, after the Christmas pageant."

Helen had given him a secretive, knowing smile. "I think tonight is gonna be chock-full of surprises. I love Christmas."

"It's the Christmas Eve performance and Heather Samuels comes down with bronchitis," Chet said, one hand on his head and the other on his stomach. "What are we gonna do, Leandra? We gotta have a solo of 'Silent Night.' It's a tradition."

They were at the civic center, getting ready for tonight's sold-out performance. Leandra didn't think she could take much more.

"I know, I know," she replied, looking down at her watch. Thirty minutes until production and now this. Heather Samuels had the voice of a pop diva and was every bit as pretty. "Is there anyone else who could possibly do it?"

"I can," a small voice said from behind her.

Leandra whirled to find Layla standing there, her big blue eyes filled with hope. "I can sing the solo, if that's okay with y'all."

"Are you sure, honey?" Chet asked, shrugging as he glanced over at Leandra. "Heather's hard to beat, what with her winning all them contests and titles and such.''

"I can do it," Layla said, her voice gaining strength. "Mrs. Flanagan—Colleen—says I have a natural talent for singing. Not that anybody at my house would notice."

Leandra knew the girl was referring to her father. She'd already heard Layla complaining that he'd stayed out in the barn most of last night. And now he was late again. Had he just gone back into his self-imposed exile rather than face the truth?

"Okay, Layla," she said, instinct telling her to give Layla a chance. "You will sing the final solo—'Silent Night.' Do you need a warm-up practice?"

Layla's smile was sheepish and shy. "I've been practicing in the bathroom already." Then she looked up at Leandra.

Leandra saw the doubt and sadness in the girl's eyes.

"What's wrong?"

Instead of answering her, Layla rushed to hug Leandra close. "We all wanted you to be our new mother. I'm sorry it didn't work out."

Leandra told herself she wouldn't cry. Yet tears pricked her eyes. "Me, too, honey."

Nate reached the auditorium a few minutes before the time for the production to start. After hurrying to get into the lion costume, he saw Leandra backstage. The look she cast toward him told him she wasn't too pleased with his being late.

And maybe he was too late. Too late to make amends with his children. Too late to heal the rift with their grandfather, something Helen had been urging him to do. And way too late to make Leandra see that he'd been the biggest kind of fool.

He just wanted to get through this, so he could make Leandra see reason. So he could tell her that he loved her.

But right now, all he could do was wait for his cue.

An hour later, Nate came back out on the stage along with all the other players. Taking his position as lion, he watched Leandra's face underneath the white fleece of her own costume. The lamb didn't look peaceful. And the lion felt like roaring his own discontent. It was time for the last solo, and Nate couldn't wait for it to be over.

''Silent Night.''

As the choir off to the right hummed and swayed, the audience members each lit their own thin white candles, passing the flame until the darkness flared brightly with hundreds of tiny beacons. Those beacons seemed to be calling to Nate.

Then with the candlelight to guide them, the angels came to watch over baby Jesus. Little Brittney sure made a beautiful angel. Even rambunctious little Philip looked angelic as he strolled onto the stage. And his own Matthew stood straight and tall, a true shepherd.

Unlike during the other performances, tonight, Nate's impatient, bruised heart seemed to fill with a joy he'd never experienced before. Alicia would be so proud of their children. And he was proud of them, too. Yet it had been a long time since he'd told them that.

Just one more thing he needed to do, to set things right again. If he could just get through this night.

Where was Heather, anyway? It was time for the solo.

And then the entire building seemed to hold its breath as one beautiful angel walked out onto the stage. Nate waited, expecting the local beauty queen to sing as she had during the other productions. But when he instead saw a beautiful blond-haired girl, dressed in flowing pink, his heart stopped.

Layla.

He must have gasped, because Leandra turned to look up at him. Nate didn't even realize he'd reached up to grasp both of Leandra's arms until he looked down and saw he was clinging to her as she stood in front of him. But he couldn't let go.

And then he heard Layla's soft sweet voice and wondered if the angels were indeed singing tonight.

As his oldest daughter sang this most holy of songs, Nate's heart let go of the last of its bitterness. All was calm, all was bright. He had a future filled with hope, and...his heart was filled with a heavenly peace.

He could almost hear Alicia's sweet words echoing in his daughter's beautiful voice.

Nate, be happy. Be strong. Be at peace. It's all right now, darling. Everything is as it should be.

When Layla finished the song, Nate fought against the tears falling down his face. He leaned toward Leandra then, his hands still gripping her arms.

"I didn't know," he said, the whisper full of an urgent tenderness. "I didn't know."

To his great relief, Leandra didn't pull away— they were onstage after all. Instead, she turned to glance up at him, her own eyes misty and brimming with tears. Then she placed a hand on his arm. "Now you do."

"That was the most beautiful—" Helen stopped, dabbing at her eyes with a tissue, her expensive white wool suit smeared with tear streaks. "Layla, darling, you are blessed with an incredible voice. What a songbird!"

Nate, still in costume, stood with his family in the hallway just beyond the stage. Pulling Layla close, he said, "Honey, I am so proud of you. Why didn't you tell me you could sing like that?"

"I tried," Layla replied, hugging him tightly.

"But I never listened, did I?"

At her muffled "No," he lifted her chin with a

thumb. "Well, from now on, things are gonna be different. I'm going to be a better father, to all of you."

"That's a start," a gruff voice said from behind him. "And I'm going to join in that promise by being a better grandfather."

Nate turned to find Davis Montgomery standing there in an expensive wool overcoat and tailored business suit.

"Hello, Nate."

Nate glanced over at Helen. "You called him."

"I surely did. Merry Christmas, Nathan."

Davis came closer, then smiled down at the three wide-eyed children standing with Nate and Helen. "Layla, I'm your grandfather Montgomery. And I just have to say that you have the voice of an angel."

"You heard me?" Layla asked, a smile brightening her face.

"I heard you." Davis extended his hand to Nate. "And if your father doesn't mind, I'd love to follow y'all home for a Christmas Eve visit."

Nate looked down at the hopeful, expectant faces of his children, then reached out to shake the other man's hand. He had to start living up to his promises and tonight was as good a time as any. "I don't mind at all. We'd be glad to have you."

"Then we'll just go on home and get the coffee started and the pecan pie cut," Helen said, grabbing

Nate by his lion's mane to turn him around. "While you take care of that...unfinished business."

Nate followed the direction of her gaze.

Leandra was watching them from the other door.

Leandra told herself to just go. Get out of this silly costume and go on home. But her family was waiting for her at the church across the street. She couldn't skip the Christmas Eve service. She needed to be with her family, now more than ever.

But Nate was waiting for her at the end of the hall.

At least, he looked like he wanted to tell her something. But then, he'd had plenty of time, all week, to talk to her.

You avoided him, remember?

She watched as he kissed his children and sent them off with Helen and their grandfather. She'd figured out the tall, distinguished-looking man must be Davis Montgomery. Would Nate turn him away, too?

It didn't look that way. Davis was laughing and talking, with Brittney up in his arms and Matt right at his heels asking questions as they left the building with Helen.

The now quiet, deserted building.

Leandra stood at one door, and Nate stood at the other.

Then he motioned for her.

And she went to him.

"Can you come out to the prayer garden with me?" he asked.

Her heart tapped at her chest like a bare branch hitting a window. "Nate, I—"

"Please?" he asked, his gaze never wavering.

In spite of the agony she felt deep inside, Leandra saw something there in his eyes. Something firm and sure. And complete.

"Let me go change," she replied, not willing to have a serious conversation in a lamb's suit.

He looked down at his own outfit. "Yeah, I guess I'd better do that myself. I'll meet you there in about five minutes."

A short time later, Leandra was dressed in her best burgundy wool Christmas dress, her black wool topper keeping the chill of the icy wind off her as she made her way over to the prayer garden. It was nearly dusk, and the church service would be starting soon, *but Nate wanted to see her.*

She kept telling herself not to get excited. *Don't let your heart do this.* He just wants to say goodbye.

That's all.

But when she looked up and saw him coming toward her in his jeans and worn leather jacket, her heart got the better of her. He was carrying a large, gift-wrapped box. And he was smiling.

"What's this?" she asked when he handed her the box. The shiny Christmas paper felt cool against her hands as she took the package.

And then it started to snow, the shimmering

flakes falling like crystallized teardrops all around them.

She held a hand up to catch a delicate snowflake. "Maybe we'd better—"

"Open it, Leandra. Before I lose my nerve."

She looked up at him, watching the tiny perfectly formed snowflakes as they hit his thick, wavy hair and settled on his bronze face. Nate ignored the snow, his gaze locked with hers, and in the silence of the white cadence, Leandra saw hope there in his eyes.

She sat down on the bench—the same bench where he'd first kissed her. With shaking hands, she tugged at the colorful holiday paper, then tried to get the box open.

"Let me help," Nate said. Bending down on one knee, he kneeled in front of her to hold the square box while she reached inside to claim her prize.

And then she saw it. A small, Victorian house. Another birdhouse. Though the churchyard lights were muted because of the falling snow, Leandra could tell this was an exact replica of his own house.

Except this one wasn't rundown or forlorn looking.

And over the doorway, there was a small gold-etched sign that read Lea's House.

"Nate," she said as she held the dainty white-and-blue house on her lap, "it's so...perfect."

"It can be," he said, still on bent knee. "If you'll still have me."

"What do you mean?"

"I mean," he said, reaching up a hand to crush her hair against her face, "that I was wrong. And I'm asking you to forgive me. I didn't tell you the truth the other night."

She leaned her head into his open hand, pressing her cheek against the warmth of his palm. Then she closed her eyes. "What is the truth, Nate?"

He urged her head up. "Look at me."

She opened her eyes then, to find him so close, his gaze holding her there.

"I love you," he said. "And…I want you to be my wife." When she tried to speak, he quieted her with a finger to her lips. "And I want you to live in a house just like this one. My house. Our house. I'm going to remodel it from basement to turret, rebuild it like I built this little house, just for you, Lea. Only you."

Leandra couldn't stop the tears from falling. Nor could she stop her next words. "But…it was Alicia's—"

"Was," he said, the one word filled with so much pain and despair, she wondered if he still had doubts himself. *"Was,"* he repeated, stronger now, his finger still brushing her lips. "But I'm okay with that—I've made my peace with the Lord. And I'm willing to show off those birdhouses, if you still have a hankering to be my marketing manager."

He moved his fingers over her face, touching on teardrops and snowflakes alike, then leaned close to give her a quick kiss. "I'm a changed man, thanks to you."

"Nate, I didn't mean to change you."

"Ah, but you did. You did. And I thank God for it. And...I want you in my life now and forever." Taking the little house from her, he placed it back in the box. "Now, what do you say? I can't offer you fancy cars and city lights, but I can offer you this love I feel with all my heart. Will you marry me?"

Before she could answer, they heard running feet moving across the parking lot. Leandra looked up to see three children barreling down on them. Three happy, grinning, blond-haired children.

"Did she say yes? Did she?" Brittney asked as she slammed into her father and sent him sprawling in the newly formed snow. "Aunt Helen told us you were gonna ask her. Can we watch?"

Matt and Layla reached them then, their faces cherry-red from the cold and their own excitement.

Layla, as usual, stood back, waiting. And behind her, Helen and Davis huddled together, brother and sister alike as their wing-tipped brows shot up in a questioning expression.

"They insisted on finding you," Helen explained with a shrug.

"Well?" Matt asked, his hands on his hips, his

head slanted at a sideways angle. "Are y'all really getting married?"

Nate, on the ground with Brittney glued to his neck, lifted his face toward Leandra. "That all depends on Leandra. Will you marry us, Miss Flanagain?"

Leandra looked down at the man at her feet, her breath catching in her throat. He sat there in the snow, with a child on his lap, looking so lovable, so honest, that she knew she couldn't ever leave his side again.

"Yes, I will marry you—y'all," she said, tears streaming down her face. "Yes."

Nate lifted himself up, holding Brittney tightly in one arm as he placed the other around Leandra and kissed her firmly.

"Thank you."

"For what?" she asked, her lips inches from his.

"For believing in me, for agreeing to be my wife. For forgiving me."

"I love you," she said.

Brittney giggled as Nate stood and held her high in the air, swinging her around in the soft, silent snowfall. "She loves us, sunshine. What do you say about that?"

Brittney smiled her delight as her father whirled her around and around. "I'm glad," she called out, enjoying the echo of her words as she flew through the air. "But I told you she was perfect, didn't I?"

"You sure did," Nate said, lifting her out over his head.

"I'm a snow angel," Brittney said, squealing in delight as she held her arms out, the snowfall hitting her face. "And I've finally got a new mommy."

"That's good enough for me," Helen said, grabbing children in both hands. "Now, Nate put that child down before you both throw up. Why don't we head back to the house for a real celebration?"

Nate dropped Brittney to her feet, caught his breath, then pulled Leandra up off the bench. He took Leandra's hand on one side and Layla's on the other. Looking back at Matt, Helen and Davis, he said, "I've got a better idea. Let's go to church."

And that's exactly what they did. As a family.

Epilogue

The next Thanksgiving…

"Leandra, thank you so much for inviting us to your home for Thanksgiving." Colleen looked down the long table at her daughter, her words lifting over the drone of many voices talking all at once.

Leandra smiled at her mother, then glanced at her husband. "Thank Nate, Mom. He's the one who insisted it was our turn to play host. I think he just wanted to show off the house."

Jack held up his tea glass. "Well, the house *is* beautiful, but I'd like to especially thank him for keeping *you* out of the kitchen. Nate, the smoked turkey and baked ham sure do look good."

Nate laughed while Leandra wagged a finger at

her brother then said, "I made the fruit salad, thank you."

Margaret bobbed her head. "I watched her. She knew exactly what she was doing."

"Just so she didn't make any of her famous dumplings," Richard said, grinning from ear to ear.

Davis Montgomery, sitting by Aunt Helen, lifted a brow. "I don't think I've ever had your dumplings, Leandra. Maybe you can whip up a batch while I'm here."

Helen, resplendent in a dark-brown sweater with a happy, grinning gold-and-orange turkey embroidered across the front, winked at Leandra, then slapped her brother on the back. "I'm sure she'd be glad to do just that, right, Lea?"

Nate smiled, then leaned over to kiss his frowning wife. "Everyone should experience your dumplings at least once, honey."

When her brothers all started snickering and hiding their grins behind their white linen napkins, Leandra couldn't resist her own smile. "Okay, enough," she replied, slamming a hand down on the Battenburg lace tablecloth. "Everyone contributed to *this* meal, and I'm just thankful that we're all here together."

"Me, too," Nate said, taking his wife's hand. "And I'd like to say grace now."

While everyone held hands around the table, and the children—Cameron and Philip, Corey, Brittney and Matt sitting at the smaller children's table, and his all-grown-up Layla sitting quietly by Mark—all closed their eyes to give thanks, Nate took a moment to reflect on the past year.

He still couldn't believe how good his life was now. He had three wonderful, healthy children and he'd inherited a large, loud, pushy, nosy, loving family when he'd married Leandra back in the spring. As he looked around at the people gathered at his dining table, Nate once again thanked God for giving him a second chance to be happy.

His children now had their Aunt Helen and their grandfather Montgomery in their lives on a regular basis. He was glad they'd come to be here today, too.

Jack and Margaret sat together by Leandra's parents. Those two had taken some time to get used to, but they'd turned out to be his closest friends. And now they had a brand-new baby daughter, Emily. Michael and Kim had accepted Nate right away. He watched as they fussed over their toddler, Carissa. Mark was still the quiet, observant one, but he'd been the best man at their wedding, and he was a good listener—and still very much single.

And Richard—Richard had helped Nate to launch Welby Woodworks by pushing Nate's designs in his store and setting up a Web site on the Internet. Now, it seemed everybody wanted a Welby birdhouse in their own home. He had orders well into next year.

Nate also owed a big thanks to Howard and Colleen Flanagan. They'd accepted his children as their own grandchildren by offering advice, baby-sitting and carpooling whenever he and Leandra were busy.

And they stayed very busy these days, what with his regular job as construction foreman and his business on the side, and her work at city hall. But they were never too busy for family. Now, Nate's after-hours work was scheduled with family in mind—the children and Leandra pitched in and helped, and kept him company while he worked. The barn was now a place for all of them to be together, not just a retreat for a man with a broken heart.

And Leandra.

Thanks to Leandra, his heart was full and happy again. And his house was built on a strong foundation of faith. Leandra had made this place a home by working tirelessly to redecorate and refurbish each and every room. Today, the whole house shined and glistened with all the colors of fall—pumpkins on the porch, gold, orange, and burgundy colored mums growing in the many flower beds and sitting in clay pots and brightly painted containers all over every available surface of the house. The Welby home was full of so much bounty—more than he ever dreamed possible.

Nate finished the prayer, then smiled at the people, the family, that filled his home on this special day. But he had one more thing to be grateful for on this Thanksgiving. Giving Leandra a questioning look, he whispered, "Can I tell them?"

"Tell us what, Daddy?" Brittney said from her spot at the children's table.

Philip grinned and swiped her roll while she wasn't looking, but a frown from his grandfather made him put it right back down.

"You've sure got big ears," Nate told his youngest daughter. "But your mom and I do have a surprise." He sent Layla a special, secret look. She already knew—they'd had a long talk last night. Her smile told him she couldn't wait to share the news with the rest of the family.

"What? What?" Brittney asked, jumping up in her chair.

"Don't knock your milk over," Nate warned. Then he turned to Leandra. The tears in her eyes only added to the glow on her face. His wife had never looked more beautiful.

"Tell them," she said, her eyes bright.

Taking her hand in his, Nate looked out over the table, took a deep breath, then said, "We're going to have a baby."

Everyone started talking at once. Margaret and Kim both got up to hug Leandra, while Howard and Colleen hugged each other and grinned. Davis and Helen gave each other a long, meaningful look, then shook hands with Leandra's parents. Brittney danced around the table, clapping her hands and squealing her delight.

"I hope it's a boy," Matt said, rolling his eyes at his sister's embarrassing display of pride.

Leandra's four brothers gave each other high fives and hooted with laughter. "She finally did it," Richard said.

"That's great," Mark added, his gaze centered on Leandra. "I'm happy for you, Sis."

Leandra wiped the tears from her eyes, then glanced out the window to the big, sunny side porch just off the dining room. "Look, Nate. The cardinals are in their house. Maybe they'll have babies soon, too."

Nate watched as the birds fussed and played on the tiny porch of the Victorian birdhouse he'd built for Leandra last Christmas. Like a beam straight from heaven, rays of noonday sunshine poured a bright golden light over the dainty little house.

Lea's house.

He'd never seen a more beautiful sight.

* * * * *

Dear Reader,

We've all made plans for ourselves only to have those plans change through circumstance. Sometimes it's hard to understand why life doesn't turn out the way we wanted. And sometimes, we find strength through adversity.

When Leandra found Nathan, he was broken in spirit and shut off from what mattered most in life—his home, his family and his faith. Leandra was beginning to discover these things were important to her. Now she had to show Nate he was still worthy of a happy home and strong faith in God.

It was wonderful to bring these two very different people together with those basic principles we all seek in our plan for life—home and family, faith and love.

God does have a plan for each of us, but we have to step out into the light and ask for his help in order to see that plan. I'm so glad Nate took that step and made a home with Leandra. Maybe you've lost your way, lost sight of God's plan for your life. If so, turn to the light and ask God to guide your way. He will direct your steps. I hope this story comforts you in your own faith journey.

Until next time, may the angels watch over you while you sleep.

Lenora Worth